MOONCHILD

Voyage of the Lost and Found

AISHA BUSHBY

EGMONT

We bring stories to life

First published in Great Britain in 2020
by Egmont Books UK Ltd,
2 Minster Court, London EC3R 7BB
www.egmontbooks.co.uk

Text copyright © 2020 Aisha Bushby
Illustration copyright © 2020 Rachael Dean

The moral rights of the author have been asserted

ISBN 9781405293211

A CIP catalogue record for this title is available from the British Library

69014/001

Printed and bound in Great Britain by CPI Group

FSC
www.fsc.org

MIX
Paper from
responsible sources
FSC® C020471

To Dad, for giving me the world.

AB

A special thank you to my two sisters, Hannah and Sarah, whose creativity and ambition have influenced me throughout my life and given me the drive I have with my work today.

RD

Beyond the Horizon

Have you ever wondered what lies just beyond the horizon?

Have you ever looked out at the sea just to watch the waves tumble over one another in a race to reach the shore? Have you looked past those waves to see the line that separates the sky from the sea?

The next time you do, you might see a glimmer of something in the distance. You'll wonder if maybe it's the light of the sun bouncing off the ocean, or a bird in flight, or maybe it was just your imagination swimming wild.

But you won't be sure.

So you'll rub your eyes and look again, just to be absolutely positive that you didn't see something. But by then it's gone.

If you've done just one of those things, then chances are you've seen the Sahar Peninsula.

Haven't heard of it? I didn't expect you to. Because this is the first time I'm sharing it with the world, and you're one of the first to find out about it.

The Sahar Peninsula is a place that lies just beyond the horizon. If you've ever tried to reach the horizon, you'll realize it isn't the easiest to get to. No maps will take you there, nor can it be charted by gazing up at the stars, or down at a compass.

But if you ever find yourself inclined to search for the Sahar Peninsula, just follow the horizon and believe. Follow it and you'll find a new part of the world that you never knew was there. Hidden, just out of sight.

It's a shy place, one that doesn't like too much attention, so don't stare at it for too long, and don't let it know that you're looking.

If you're wondering who I am, and why I'm telling you this story, you'll have to wait for quite some time to find out. It's a secret, you understand. And I need to know that you're the right person to keep it.

Are you?

I'm not so sure just yet.

Now that we've introduced ourselves, shall we begin?

Chapter 1

The dhow's sail flapped like the wings of a giant bird, and the mast creaked and moaned against the wind. The cabin was louder and more crowded than usual with the chickens and pregnant goat all tied to posts for safety. They cried out, confused.

The barometer spun wildly, unable to read the shift in the storm. But Namur, Amira's *jinni*, could. He had been acting strangely for days. He seemed to know why the wind howled like a mournful wolf; why the lightning struck, and the thunder clapped; he seemed to see something more than clouds and rain. Something *beyond*.

But right now Namur was missing. And it felt as if a needle had pierced right through Amira's heart. She would have to leave the safety of the cabin to find him, abandoning the animals she had promised to keep safe – though she knew, with certainty, that she would travel to the very ends of the earth for him. She would travel all the way to the moon, if she had to.

Namur was hers, after all, and she was his.

Amira and Namur had been born together in a giant oyster. Her sea witch mothers were fishing one day and they'd caught it – pale blue and purple – and pulled it from the sea.

They had told her she was a gift, and so was Namur. And, from then on, they were a family.

Amira and Namur had grown together from a baby and kitten. They had sailed their first voyage together, taken their first steps on land and they would brave this storm together, as always.

Once outside Amira peered across the length of the dhow, but it was difficult to see through the rain that pelted her hard.

'Amira!' Dunya, her mother, called out. She was struggling to steer them away from the rocks that poked out of the ocean, like clawed hands waiting to take hold of the dhow and drag it under. 'What are you doing?'

'Namur's missing!' cried Amira. 'I lost him when I was tying up the animals. I have to find him.'

Dunya's response was lost to the wind as Amira pressed

on, a rope tied round her waist.

Her other mother, Jamila, had just managed to pull the sail down to stop it catching in the wind, face determined, long hair billowing behind her. Still the storm raged on, and the clouds covered the sky like a blanket.

Amira took one step, then two, and stumbled, her knees landing hard on the wooden floor. The dhow tilted, and Amira slid all the way down it, crashing into the side. Her shoulder throbbed with pain, shooting all the way down her arm, though she barely felt it. The pain inside her, the fear of losing Namur, was greater.

'Land ho!' called Jamila, from above.

Amira turned to look at where her mother was pointing and found a tiny dot in the distance the size of a dung beetle. Land was good. It meant they had a chance at getting out of the storm. But first she had to find Namur.

She stood up just as the dhow tilted in the other direction, swaying to and fro like a toy rocking horse. But she was ready this time.

Amira braced herself, leaning her body in the opposite direction to keep balanced. It worked. The dhow righted itself for a moment, and Amira took her chance to run across to the bow.

'Namur!' she called, frantically searching. 'Namur!' Tears streaked her face, mingling with the rain and the salty sea spray.

What if he had fallen off? What would she do if she lost her *jinni*?

'Namur!' Amira cried for the third time, sobbing now.

It was all her fault. She had left the cabin door open as the dhow began to tilt, and she had watched in horror as Namur slid outside – desperately trying to grip the slippery wood with his claws – before disappearing from sight.

Though they shared a connection, their fates were separate, which meant Amira could tread her own path, and Namur his. But Amira knew she would fight for him always, and that's why she had plunged into the uncertainty of the storm.

After a few moments of nothing but wind and rain, Namur miaowed so quietly Amira almost didn't hear him.

'Where are you?' she asked desperately, following the sound of his voice. The wind was playing tricks on her ears, carrying her *jinni*'s voice left and right.

'There you are!' called Amira at last, barely able to speak.

Namur was crouched beneath the rowing boat, ears pinned back, nose dripping. He was a small striped cat with big green eyes, like emeralds, and fur that glinted in the darkness of the storm.

'My rope won't reach that far,' Amira explained. 'You'll have to run to me.'

She took her jacket off, not caring that she was getting wetter by the second, and held it out for Namur. He leaned back on shaking legs and leaped into her arms, shivering, his fur matted with rain. Namur let out another distressed miaow and Amira clicked her tongue to soothe him, wrapping him in the jacket.

'It's OK,' she said, nuzzling him. 'You're OK now.'

Amira began to make her way back across to the safety of the cabin below, Namur bundled in her arms. Both of her mothers were steering together now. Jamila yelled something, her eyes wide and fearful. It sounded like a warning, but Amira couldn't quite hear.

The wind was blowing against Amira now, lashing her in the face. Walking back was like wading through sand. The storm flung her around as if she were nothing but a feather.

After the third step Amira dropped her jacket – and Namur, who was bundled inside.

'No!' she screamed as her jacket fell off the side of the dhow.

Amira ran to the railings and looked out at the ocean. She saw her jacket floating at the surface of the water, pulled in all directions. Within seconds it was swallowed up by the waves.

'Namur!' screamed Amira. 'Namur!'

A sharp tug pulled her back with force.

Amira turned and was immediately cocooned into Jamila's arms, her mother's long hair tickling her face as she screamed into Amira's ear: 'There's a wave coming, Amira, a big one. You have to go inside. Now!'

'No!' Amira screamed back, pulling herself free. She began to untie herself from the rope that held her waist, pushing her mother away. She would not be stopped.

Amira was almost free, ready to jump overboard, when she looked down to see Namur climbing up the side of the dhow, using their fishing net as his ladder. He sprang aboard and crouched by her feet, shivering.

'How did y—' Amira began to ask, but her words were

cut short.

The sky darkened even more as a wave twice the height of the dhow came towards them at full speed. Amira bundled Namur into her arms again, and Jamila dragged them both into the cabin, slamming the door firmly behind them.

Amira heard the wave before she felt it. A low rumbling, the force of it enough to shatter the dhow as if it were nothing more than an eggshell. She closed her eyes and nuzzled into Namur, the scent of his fur sweet, like honey.

For a brief moment, the world fell silent.

Then Amira heard Dunya yell from the deck. 'She's ready! We can drive her straight into the wave.'

The unmistakable sound of sea and wind tore through the cracks in the wood, and Dunya's voice was gone.

A second passed.

Then two.

The wave swallowed the dhow whole, and Amira's world turned upside down.

Chapter 2

I imagine you are wondering what happened that night on the dhow. Did the group survive the storm? Well, that would be telling, wouldn't it?

I've not yet decided which part of this story to tell (because stories never start at the beginning and they never ever finish at the end), or if, indeed, I should be telling this story at all. Wouldn't you rather know about the time Amira and Namur escaped a flight of rocs? Or, perhaps, about the time they had to rescue the goat, Ramady, from drowning?

No? You'd rather discover their fate on the dhow? Well, that's a risk you'll have to take, for some stories are longer than others, and some more perilous. And this one, depending on the fate of our two friends, might end up rather short and tragic indeed.

But, if you're still sure, absolutely sure, then we really

must start at the *very* beginning . . .

Jinn were born at the dawn of time, taking the form of an animal of their choosing.

Together with humans they created a balance, a harmony in the world, and other creatures grew and thrived because of them. For many years there was peace. But things, as you know, can often go wrong. Some creatures are born from darkness, and, as they grow, they spread fear and hatred.

But this isn't a story about *those* creatures. Not yet, anyway. It is a story about *jinn*.

Many believe *jinn* exist in the realm of the dark; they believe them to be creatures of shadow and night. But those people are wrong. Do not listen to them.

The *jinn* exist at the very edges of our realm, in a place most people don't think to look. And the children who welcome the *jinn* have access to this realm. You'll discover this yourself, when we return to Amira and Namur's story.

But before we do, I want to ask you some questions.

Have you ever felt a tingling sensation at the back of

your neck? Has something ever grazed against your cheek, but you couldn't find the source? Have you ever felt a shiver down your spine that came as if from nowhere?

If any of those things have happened, you have felt the presence of your very own *jinni*.

They will appear to you when you most need them. And only you can truly know when that is.

But this, the story of you and your own *jinni*, is one you must discover for yourself. And trust me: there will be time. But now we have a rather more pressing story waiting for us on the very next page.

Shall I return to Amira and Namur now? Shall I reveal their fate on that wild and stormy night?

Well, if you're sure, let's continue . . .

Chapter 3

'You shouldn't do that when you're in such a foul mood,' warned Jamila. 'You'll pass it on.'

Amira, who had been knotting tapestries made of brown cord, stopped, folded her arms, and glared at her mother.

'It's hard to be in a good mood,' she said. 'When the cabin smells so much like . . . like –'

'Like what?' Jamila interrupted irritably. 'You've been complaining about the smell for days. We can't exactly change it, can we?'

The dhow's cabin was small, with a low table at its centre. Instead of chairs, there were sequined cushions, well worn. The walls were covered in ivy, and in tapestries knotted over the years. Jars of tonics and cordials hung from bags in odd places, and stacks of books lined each corner of the room.

'It smells like sand and something sharp.' Amira sighed,

sinking down on to one of the cushions tucked beneath the low table. 'Like everything is crumbling around us. It's stifling. I can't *breathe* half the time.'

Two round windows showed views of the horizon on one side, and a busy port on the other. Amira longed to be outside, exploring, but their dhow had been damaged in the storm, and they had to fix it.

Amira had the unusual ability to read the emotions of those around her, like the pages of a book. But the emotions didn't appear to her as words; they appeared as smells, and occasionally visions.

Some emotions, often the positive ones, have a single smell, or vision, attached to them. Others, the more complicated emotions, the darker ones buried deep, are like a sickly feast. Excitement is like a freshly baked cake slathered in honey. Love is sugary sweets, boiled and cooled. But the emotions on the dhow, ever since the storm had plunged them into uncertainty, were like the air after a sandstorm. And Amira couldn't see beyond the haze to understand them.

Jamila, who had been mixing cordials at the table, stopped what she was doing and turned to her daughter, her voice a little softer this time.

'It's difficult,' she began. 'We were so lucky not to have lost anyone in that storm. But, as you know, we were close.'

She glanced to where Namur was perched on Amira's shoulders. Namur's paws were tucked beneath Amira's chin, tail wrapped round her neck. Amira swallowed, her mouth suddenly dry. She tried not to think about the day she almost lost her *jinni*.

Namur's pure form was invisible. And most of the time Amira could feel him more than see him: the weight of his body on her shoulders, the tickle of his fur on her neck, the gentle vibrations of his purrs. Even when he wasn't on her shoulders, she could sense him. And she could feel it when he was gone too. It felt like hunger and emptiness.

Namur appeared whenever Amira was angry. Which, if you knew Amira at all, was a lot of the time. His bones would form first, followed by flesh, skin and fur. The entire process was rather gruesome and took a full minute to complete. The last part of him to appear was the soft glow that haloed his fur, like a moon ring, setting him apart from normal animals.

But ever since the dhow had sailed into the storm, Namur hadn't turned invisible once.

Amira stared out of the window as night crept towards them like a hunting scorpion. In the distance she saw a cluster of orange and pink clouds emerge from the horizon resembling a row of mountains.

Odd, she thought. Usually clouds came down from the sky, not up from the sea.

Namur hopped from her shoulder on to the windowsill, his tail swishing left and right as he peered into the distance. Every few moments he let out a low growl, as if remembering what had happened the night of the storm.

Thunder, followed by lightning, struck three times before Amira spoke.

'I need to tell you something,' Amira blurted, steering the conversation like a rogue dhow.

'What is it?' asked Jamila distractedly. She was back to mixing, adding a pinch of rosemary to a green bottle filled with a smoking liquid.

'I've started my . . . blood cycle,' said Amira, her face heating up. She tore her eyes away from the window, from the lingering storm, but couldn't quite look at her mother. She focused her attention instead on the large red-velvet cushion she was sitting on, fiddling with its delicate black tassels.

'When?' asked Jamila, sounding surprised.

'The day the storm hit. I was going to tell you sooner, but then . . .'

Namur watched Amira's hands, his head turning with her every movement. He jumped off her shoulders to inspect the cushion tassels more closely.

Though *jinn* are spirits, not animals, they adopt the characteristics of the creatures whose forms they choose to take. Namur, for example, loved milk and stealing pieces of chicken from under Jamila's nose. He loved having his ear scratched, but only the left one. And his favourite possession in the entire world was a tattered old belt of Amira's. Any time anyone picked it up, his eyes turned wild.

Jamila abandoned her cordial-mixing again and turned her attention to her daughter. 'I see.'

Amira watched the concern emanating from her, like steam from a pot of soup.

'Well,' Jamila finally said, breaking the silence. 'You *are* twelve, I suppose. It was bound to happen.'

Amira sighed. 'But why is it so . . . awful and . . . painful?'

Jamila pulled her in for a hug. 'I know, my darling,' she said. 'It isn't pleasant at all. But trust me when I say you will get used to it.'

'Really?' asked Amira, pulling back to face her mother.

'Absolutely.'

Jamila's voice was an octave too high, and her smile a little too practised. Amira could taste the deceit, like sour milk. It was tinged with layers of other flavours, unique to their conversation, and it lingered even as the conversation moved on.

'You're *lying*,' Amira declared.

'No, I'm not.'

Amira held her mother's gaze like a predator stalking its prey. Jamila's lips flickered like the wings of a butterfly, and she smiled guiltily. Within seconds, that smile turned to laughter. Amira joined in, like the next note in a happy song.

Namur, who had been inspecting Jamila's cordial on

the table, turned to them both quizzically.

'Ow, stop!' begged Amira, hands wrapped round her stomach. 'It hurts to laugh.' But she felt lighter than she had in days.

'Let's get you a soothing tonic,' said Jamila, clapping her hands before returning to a task she knew better than any other – mixing.

Jamila didn't usually mix antidotes for headaches or stomach ailments. She sold antidotes to the pains of the mind and heart. A cordial, blended with goat's milk, to ease the worries that come before sleep; a tonic, taken at dawn, to soften the pain of losing the one you love most; a mixture, rubbed into the temples, to help the flow of happy thoughts.

Of course, unlike the pains of the body, the woes of the mind and heart are much more difficult to fix. They don't simply disappear, but fade; and often time is the best cure of all.

'Sometimes, Amira,' Jamila mused, handing her a mug filled with a steaming brown liquid that looked entirely unappealing, 'I think your truth-smelling abilities do more harm than good.'

'So you *were* lying?' said Amira, crawling on to her mother's lap like she was six and not twelve. She blew into her mug until the drink cooled enough to sip it.

Jamila sighed. 'Yes,' she admitted. 'I was. Now, drink up. It'll make the truth much easier to stomach.'

After a moment or two, footsteps sounded overhead, loud and purposeful.

'That'll be your mother, marching like a proud horse,' Jamila muttered, before adding, 'she'll be absolutely *thrilled* with the news. Prepare yourself.'

Dunya entered the cabin, followed by the pregnant goat, who scrambled into the corner and settled down with her back to the room.

'Ramady's going to give birth in the next fortnight,' said Dunya by way of greeting her family. 'I sold seven tonics and read five palms. Rather a good day. A few others asked for their cards, so I'll do that tomorrow. People are seeking solace after the storm.' She looked sympathetic as she flung her shoes aside and dumped her bags on the table. 'Though, to be honest –'

She paused for a moment, glancing between her wife and daughter. 'Why am I speaking to myself?'

'Because you hardly took a breath to let us respond,' Jamila teased. 'Amira, would you like to tell your mother, or shall I?'

'Tell me what?' Dunya asked shrilly. 'What's happened now? We can't take any more bad luck!'

Jamila walked over to her wife and clasped Dunya's hands in her own. 'It's nothing *bad*,' she clarified. 'Amira's started her cycle.'

'What cycle? Her blood – Oh! Oh my goodness!' Dunya clapped her hands together and pulled Amira in for a hug that sang of celebration and joy. 'What a happy day!'

From behind Dunya's back, Jamila rolled her eyes playfully at Amira as she tidied up after her wife.

'Well, then, it's time,' Dunya declared.

'Time for what?' asked Amira, curiously, pulling back from her mother.

'Time you attended the souk!'

Amira grinned. 'Really? I can go?'

'Only if your mother agrees.'

'Can I, please?' Amira pleaded with Jamila.

The family of sea witches travelled for months at sea, stopping briefly at islands in the Sahar Peninsula to trade their skills for food and clothes. Amira had been allowed to play on the islands they visited, but never before had she attended a souk. Every morning they were ashore, as the sun kissed the horizon, Amira watched Dunya disappear into the crowd, a bag of magical offerings in hand. And she had always wondered what it would be like to converse with strangers and share her skills.

'I –' Jamila paused, chewing the inside of her mouth. ' – think it's time,' she eventually agreed, to Amira's surprise.

'Wonderful,' said Dunya. 'We'll start tomorrow!'

Amira's heart soared like a bird in flight as she imagined what it would be like. The people, the food, the buildings –

'On one condition,' said Jamila.

Amira's hopes landed with a thud.

'You *don't* leave your mother's side.'

Dunya nodded. 'That sounds fair, doesn't it, Amira?'

'Yes!' Amira said quickly, even though she had hoped she might be able to wander with Namur. At least she would get the chance to leave the cabin for a while. And perhaps her mothers would change their minds, if she proved herself up to the task.

Later that night, when the moon was at its highest and the lingering clouds had faded into the darkness, Amira and her mothers gathered for a story.

Jamila lit a wooden pot with perfumed wood chips and coal, and immediately the room was coated in the scent of wood and rose and orange.

'It's your turn, I think,' Dunya said to Amira, sliding the pot towards her. It was lined with silver and covered in pearls, each of them shimmering in the semi-darkness.

Amira grinned. 'I've been saving this one!' she said excitedly, standing up and dancing round the room with the pot in her hands. The smoke settled above them in a haze.

'Well, go on,' Jamila encouraged.

'Do you remember the time we visited the island of rocs?' Amira asked, returning to her seat and placing the pot between them. Her mothers nodded.

'How could we forget?' Dunya laughed.

'It happened two summers ago. . .' Amira began, and steadily the smoke began to take shape in the form of her story, colours bleeding through it as if by magic.

While Amira told her story, the smoke settled into the shape of *Tigerheart*, as it glided across the ocean.

The Sea Witch, her Jinni and the Roc Egg

A young sea witch and her cat *jinni* sailed to a beautiful island filled with trees the height of buildings and waterfall lagoons filled with mermaids. But the most magnificent thing about this island was that it was home to a flight of rocs.

The roc, if you did not know, is a giant bird with feathers as red as fire and as golden as the sun. They can grow so large that their wings span three times the length of a dhow; and their power is so great that they can swoop down and grab a full-grown elephant, taking it back to their nest to feed their young.

The island was home to twelve rocs, and they all nested peacefully together. They spent their days flying from island to island to hunt for food, sometimes snatching a shark from the ocean whenever they appeared too close to the surface. By night they would return to feed their young and protect their unhatched eggs.

The sea witch and her *jinni* were not afraid of the rocs. The great birds would never waste their energy on them. It would be, for us, like spending hours foraging, only to return with a single berry, or two.

It was a warm afternoon. The sea witch and her *jinni* had several lazy hours ahead of them, while their mothers rested and restocked the dhow. And so they decided to explore. But in order to cross to the forest and reach the lagoon – where they hoped to spy some mermaids – they were first tasked with making it past six nests which lay on the beach. Each nest was filled with three golden eggs, almost ready to hatch, and each egg was as large as the sea witch herself.

The rocs were all away hunting, and so the sea witch and her *jinni* inspected their nests, which were built from tree branches and leaves. They climbed up and stroked the eggs, which were as hard as the mast that carried their sail, but as light as sea foam.

They next ventured into the forest in search of the waterfall and the mermaids who lived in the lagoon beneath it. The forest was eerily quiet. Not a creature stirred, and the sea witch feared they would never find the lagoon. *Perhaps*, she thought, *it was just a story.*

The sea witch and her *jinni* walked and walked for what seemed like hours, with only the crunch of their footsteps for company. But they could not find the lagoon. They were close to giving up – it would be dark soon, after all – when the sound of singing stopped them in their tracks.

'Do you hear that, Namur?' said the sea witch. 'It's beautiful.'

It was as lovely as the sound of waves breaking on the shore, or the first cry of a bird in the early hours of the morning.

The *jinni* leaped from the sea witch's shoulders and darted into the trees, intent on chasing the voice.

'Namur!' the sea witch called, following the soft padding of his feet.

The sea witch realized, too late, that they had been standing near a muddy bank, which led to a fast-moving stream. She peered down to find her *jinni* bobbing up and down in the water, crying for help.

'Hold on, Namur!' the sea witch cried, and she leaped into the stream after him.

The water was cool, and ordinarily she would have enjoyed it, had they not been dragged towards the edge of a waterfall. With her *jinni* bundled in her arms, the sea witch closed her eyes, and prepared for her fate.

The singing drew closer, growing louder, but the sea witch's screams were louder still as she toppled over the waterfall, landing in the very depths of a lagoon.

Once in the water she opened her eyes to see the shape of nimble tails darting left and right, circling her like sharks. The sea witch, who was a strong swimmer, kicked against the bed of the lagoon and shot up, up, up to the surface. Then she swam to land and crawled on to a mound of grass.

There, resting on a large rock at the edge of the lagoon, were three mermaids. Sisters. But these weren't the mermaids she had read about in story books, or heard about in legends. Their faces were iridescent and scaly, and their teeth as sharp as knives. Still, the sea witch didn't fear them. She knew from experience that wicked creatures often came in the prettiest of packages, and sharp teeth and scales were not always to be feared.

And she was right. The mermaids greeted her as their own.

'Where are all the animals on this island?' the sea witch asked, while they shared a platter of fish.

'The rocs ate them,' said the first sister, rather sullenly.

'We've been so lonely without friends,' the second added.

The sea witch looked on with sympathy. 'Sometimes I get lonely on the dhow,' she admitted for the first time. 'I would like to make friends my age.'

'But you have a *jinni*,' the third one said, scratching Namur behind the ears. 'You're so very *lucky*.'

The sea witch agreed that she was, and she wanted to share some of that luck. 'How can I help?' she asked, keen to impress her new friends.

The three sisters exchanged a look.

'There is one thing . . .' said the first mermaid.

'But it's too much . . .' the second one added.

'What is it?' the sea witch answered. 'I'll do anything to help!'

'Anything?' the third mermaid asked, leaning forward hungrily.

'Well, if you *insist*,' said the first mermaid. 'Sister, would you like to explain?'

'Of course, sister,' the second mermaid answered. 'We can't leave this lagoon, because we haven't any legs to climb out. But *you* can.'

'We've been stuck here all alone for years,' the third mermaid continued. 'But if you could bring us a roc egg from the beach, we could hatch it and raise it as our own.'

'And when it is old enough, it could fly us away from this island to the sea,' the first mermaid finished dreamily.

'We have dreamed of the sea for so long,' the second mermaid explained.

The sea witch nodded. She understood their predicament. Still, it wouldn't be an easy task. The eggs were large, and the rocs dangerous. But, she reasoned to herself, the adult birds were away hunting. And they wouldn't miss one unhatched egg, would they?

'I'll do it,' the sea witch said resolutely. 'But first we need something to replace the egg, so the rocs don't realize until it's too late.'

'I know!' said the second mermaid. 'What about a large pebble?'

They all agreed that this was the best option.

Back at the beach, the sea witch and her *jinni* found the perfect pebble. They used honey from a nearby hive to paint it golden, just like the other eggs.

The sea witch and her *jinni* returned to the mermaids with a single roc egg, as promised. They dropped it into the stream and let it drift over the waterfall and into the lagoon. It landed with a splash. And together, the mermaids placed it in a nest they had already prepared, just by the side of the lagoon.

As the sea witch and her *jinni* waved goodbye to the mermaids, they could not have foreseen the trouble that would come their way . . .

◇ ✦ ◇

'You did what?' asked Jamila, horrified.

'Did the mermaids ever get out?' Dunya asked at the same time. 'And what happened to the sea witch and her *jinni?*'

'I think we *know* what happened to the sea witch,' Jamila snapped. 'Maybe you shouldn't be allowed to go to the souk, Amira, if stealing doesn't bother you . . .'

'It was a story!' insisted Amira, which wasn't a complete

lie. She hoped her mothers wouldn't pry further and find out it was real.

Jamila narrowed her eyes. 'Hmmm . . .'

'But what *did* happen to the mermaids?' Dunya persisted.

'Not now!' Jamila scolded her wife, guiding her to their cabin. 'You both need to get some rest. You have a long day ahead of you.'

Amira grinned at Dunya. 'I guess you'll have to find out another time.'

Later that night, when Amira had finally fallen asleep, she dreamed of sand and souks and the feeling of land beneath her feet.

Chapter 4

The next morning Amira rushed through her chores before sunrise. She laid out a fresh pile of grains for Ramady in the corner of the main cabin, which the goat had boldly claimed as her own. Ramady opened her eyes briefly when she approached, turning lazily from Amira to the grains, before deciding on sleep. Even the hens were confused, hesitantly plucking at their feed in the dark.

'Ready?' Dunya asked a short time later, brushing back her wet hair.

Unlike Jamila's long, curly, waves, Dunya's hair was short and straight, falling just below her ears. And, where Jamila was strong and tall, Dunya was sharp of the mind and tongue.

Amira fell somewhere in between her mothers. She looked much more like Jamila, and they shared the same temperament, but her spirit was Dunya through and through. She hoped, one day, to be captain just like her mother. She had been working hard on deck to prove her skills, and had studied every form of navigation there was.

Amira was ready for their next voyage, to prove all she had learned. But first they had to fix the dhow. And to do that they had to sell items at the souk.

'Almost,' said Amira. 'Have you seen my jacket?'

Dunya shook her head, frowning. 'No. Why?'

I laid it out last night, on top of my trousers. But this morning . . .' A spark of irritation flared inside of Amira. She toppled tables and flipped cushions in search of it. 'Never mind,' she said at last, focusing her attention on the bag of treasures she had packed for the day.

There were tapestries that Amira had knotted into shapes of flowers and birds; vials of tonics and cordials from Jamila; and Dunya's tarot cards, which she would use for her readings at the stall.

Dunya had drawn the cards herself, themed to the sea. The ink had faded, after years of passing through thousands of hands, and the edges were worn, but Dunya said that made them even more powerful. They stored the hopes and dreams of those who had used them before, and passed them on for luck.

It was the same reason Jamila had told Amira not to make her tapestries while she was in a bad mood. It wasn't kind to pass that mood on to others.

Dunya led the way to the deck, and Amira followed, marching in time with her.

'Are you coming?' she asked Namur at the cabin door.

Her *jinni* was busy lounging on one of the cushions, paws outstretched. He lifted his head and glared at her. He didn't much like mornings, and he seemed annoyed at having his sleep disturbed.

'Well?' asked Amira, hands on her hips.

Namur stood up and, very slowly, stretched and yawned, before padding over to her.

'Come on,' Amira said, rolling her eyes, as he leaped on to her shoulders. 'Don't you like adventures any more?'

◊✦◊

The port was busy that day, and it was scorching hot already. People rushed from one corner to the next, like ants scurrying across a path. Amira wondered where they were going, where they had come from, and why they were in such a rush.

The town was built on a hill. The port was at the very bottom of the hill, with palm trees lining the street and sandy houses snaking up and away from the water, piling on top of one another. In the distance were bigger buildings, with round roofs and diamond patterns carved into wooden walls.

As they stepped off the dhow, the seagulls greeted Amira, and she greeted them back. But it wasn't long before she began to feel a little peculiar. At first she thought it was her blood cycle – she had been feeling a little faint lately – but she quickly realized it was something more.

Each step felt heavy, like Amira's feet were strapped to rocks, and she began to feel queasy. After a moment, she stopped to sit at the edge of the port, facing the water. Namur climbed down, resting beside her. Amira watched the waves lash against the base of the dhow. The storm was further out today, but the sea was as wild as ever.

After several long, uncomfortable moments, Amira was violently sick into the ocean.

Namur nuzzled his head into her armpit while Dunya rubbed her back. Amira was sick once more. Eventually, Amira stood up shakily and turned to her mother.

'W-why did that happen?' she groaned, barely able to get her words out.

'Land sickness,' said Dunya, pulling a face. 'It's awful, isn't it?'

Amira grimaced, too ill to speak again.

'Do you want to get back on the dhow? Try again tomorrow?'

'N-no!' said Amira, fists clenched. 'I'm . . . OK . . . I . . . swear.'

But she wasn't. First her best jacket had gone missing, and now this. How was Amira supposed to help run her mother's stall at the souk if she couldn't even walk properly?

Dunya raised her eyebrows. 'You . . . don't . . . sound . . . OK.'

Amira laughed, which led very abruptly to a third wave of sickness.

'I'm better now,' she promised, when she was done. She filled a pouch with sea water, for luck, and stood up on shaky legs. 'Let's go.'

❖

The sounds and smells of the souk beckoned Amira

before the sights did. Conversation rose and fell like the gentle rocking of a dhow, and very occasionally laughter broke through the rhythm, like a dolphin breaching the water. The smells were intoxicating, but it wasn't the food Amira was drawn to. It was the emotions. Excitement, unlike any she had experienced before, mingled with despair, came to her as sweet as mangoes and as salty as the sea. The island was so full of life, Amira wondered whether her senses could take it.

'Are you well enough to work today?' asked Dunya, watching her closely. 'It won't be easy.'

Amira nodded, though she wasn't entirely sure if that was the truth. She was glad her mother couldn't smell *her* emotions. Namur's claws dug painfully into her shoulders, but Amira didn't complain. He seemed as uncomfortable as she did. And yet she was hungry for more. They both were.

As they turned a corner, Amira's eyes fell on a clearing filled with more people than she had ever seen before. Tables with cloth ceilings lined up together to form narrow pathways for buyers to slither through, a sky of silk protecting them from the sun. Jewels and food, embroidered blankets and cloth, hypnotized them all, drawing them close. The souk was like walking into a different realm, one that existed inside a treasure chest.

Amira could hardly blink for fear of missing it. She almost forgot her dizziness. But the emotions were many, and as Amira made her way to the heart of the souk, she could no longer decipher each one. It was like standing in the middle of a feast, hundreds of dishes mingling together.

'This is ours,' said Dunya, weaving through the crowds. She had hardly stepped behind their stall when a woman approached, asking Dunya to read her cards.

'Of course,' said Dunya without hesitation. 'You were here yesterday, weren't you? Have a shuffle of the cards and get comfortable.' She pulled up a chair so the woman could sit across from her. 'Amira, could you set the bottles on the table and hang the tapestries so they're in plain sight?'

The woman smelled of lavender, soft and fragrant, though there was something sharp resting just beneath the surface, like biting into a slice of lemon. She gave Amira a smile, but Amira was too nervous to return it. She rarely met new people.

Dunya was lighting coals topped with scented wood chips, just like they had the night before as Amira had shared her story. When Dunya was done, and the smoke had settled, she asked, 'What is it you're looking for today?'

'I have a decision to make,' the woman explained. 'And I need . . .'

Her voice faded into the cacophony of the souk. Stallholders yelled prices at the crowds that flocked to their tables like hungry gulls. The crowds yelled lower prices back. Amira also heard them discuss, in hushed whispers, the aftermath of the storm.

They spoke of land masses sinking into the ocean, and dhows disappearing at sea; they spoke of the clouds that had appeared in the distance, and neighbours packing up to stay with family inland. They said words like 'magic' and 'curse', all while looking around in the hope that no one would hear. But Amira couldn't believe that magic would cause harm. It was something to cherish, not to fear.

A few people stopped at Dunya's stall as the day went by, mostly to browse the bottles before leaving. Amira heard a few of them claim that they were 'lies', while others muttered the word 'witch' as if it were a profanity and not simply a profession. When Dunya was free, she spoke to customers with an ease Amira was sure she would never master herself.

'What is it you do?' Dunya asked one man, a canvas of wrinkles framing his lifeless eyes. He was browsing the tonics, though he seemed uncertain, as if he were afraid they might poison him.

'I am a fisherman,' he replied, and they fell into a conversation about sailing and storms.

Amira, absently stroking Namur's fur as he lay across from her on the table, couldn't help noticing a strange smell that emanated from the man. It was dark, and sickly, but not like honey and sweet fruit; it was the sort of smell that seeped beneath your fingernails and into your bones. It smelled of pain, and longing, and being lost at sea.

Amira couldn't explain it, but she feared for the man. She peered at the tonics Jamila had prepared and found one that read: *A cordial, taken with coffee, to soothe thoughts of sadness.* She picked it up and held it wordlessly in front of the man.

The man took the bottle from Amira, his calloused hands brushing over hers. He squinted as he read the bottle, and then he turned to Amira, his eyes watery and wide. 'Thank you,' he said. He glanced between her and Namur, and there was a glimmer of hope in his eyes.

Amira gave him the smile the woman had passed on to her, and he took it and wore it like a cloak in the rain. He left the souk and walked back towards the port, the bottle clutched firmly in his hands.

Amira watched him dart away into gaps in the crowd. She wondered what the old man's story was.

Because, you see, we all have our stories.

Some are bigger than others, some more perilous. But no matter the shape or size, each one is important. They have a small part of us in them, after all, a small root of our lives that can grow into the tallest tree. And if we continue to feed them, water them, let the sun warm them occasionally, they may even grow all the way to the moon.

Chapter 5

Word spread that Amira knew exactly the sort of tonic or cordial people needed to fix their problems, and they flocked to the stall like hungry fish to bait. But their emotions were overpowering, and she struggled to separate them all. Their sadness came in waves of rotten eggs and burnt coffee; their fears as overripe fruit and stale bread; and their joy as fresh flowers and sugar.

People are often unaware of their emotions. They bury them deep, like items lost in a shipwreck. They hope that if they can hide them away no one will notice, and they will disappear. But debris from shipwrecks often washes up to shore when we least expect it to. And that is precisely why Dunya and Amira had sold all of their tonics and cordials by noon.

'Amira,' said Dunya, wiping beads of sweat from her forehead. 'I need you and Namur to go back to the dhow and grab some more mixes.' Before Amira could respond,

Dunya turned to another customer, greeting them in the very same breath.

'She's letting us go on our own, Namur,' whispered Amira to her *jinni* as she readied her things. She wasn't sure she knew the way back. The houses around the souk were built like the walls of a maze, but Amira wanted to prove that she could navigate land as well as she could chart stars and read a compass at sea.

Namur, who had fallen asleep at some point between the sale of their first tonic and their last, stood up, stretched his paws and yawned. Amira leaned forward and he climbed on to her shoulders again, his whiskers tickling her cheeks.

Amira was never truly alone when Namur was around, which was why she didn't much mind being angry a lot of the time. It was his company that made her brave enough to wave Dunya goodbye and dive into the bustling crowds of the souk, back towards the port.

◇✦◇

Jamila was thrilled to find out they were doing so well at the souk. She stuffed dozens more cordials and tonics into Amira's bag.

'At this rate, we'll be able to leave within the week!' she said. 'Oh, and tell your mother Ramady is being an absolute nightmare today. You'd think she was giving birth to the next queen, the way she's acting.'

Amira peered across the cabin to see the pregnant goat watching her with suspicion. She had managed to pull all of the floor cushions so they surrounded her like a velvet moat.

'Don't even *think* about crossing the boundary,' Jamila warned when Amira stepped closer.

Ramady was sitting on a pile of clothes she had, presumably, collected herself. She snapped when Amira tried to reach in and claim them back.

'Told you,' said Jamila.

'Is that my best jacket?' asked Amira, turning to her mother, scandalized. 'I thought I'd lost it!'

She tried to fathom how a goat could've opened her bedroom door. If she didn't know better, she would've suspected Ramady was a *jinni* too.

'You don't want to see what she did to my favourite boots,' said Jamila with a shudder. And Amira could swear she saw a single tear slide down her mother's face.

As Amira wandered back through the labyrinthine streets towards the souk again, she stopped to take in the houses huddled together like friends sharing secrets on a cold winter's night. Namur was just as curious. Together they peered into open doors and windows, glimpsing the lives of those on land. In one house three children played together, escaping the sun, while their father hung clothes up outside the window. Amira had never really spared a thought for fathers. From what she could see, they seemed no different to mothers.

In the alleyways they found neighbours knocking on

doors, sharing gossip; friends marching along, arms linked, ready to explore the souk; and people hurrying from one place to the next like dhows chasing the wind.

It was only when they lost sight of the sea, with no sounds of the souk ahead, that Amira realized they were lost. Her heartbeat picked up pace, and her body tingled with nerves. She had never been lost before.

'What do we do, Namur?' she asked, twisting around in panic.

Namur lifted his head up and sniffed at the air. For a moment he looked as if had caught wind of something. Was it the smells of the souk? But then he sneezed and settled back on Amira's shoulders.

What if she retraced her steps back to the dhow, and started again? Amira turned, searching for the alley she had just exited, and rushed back. In her haste she forgot to look to her left. And that was why she crashed into someone coming the other way.

The force of the collision knocked her to the floor. The bottles of tonic and cordial cracked, their contents spilling everywhere, sizzling on the hot ground.

Confusingly, Amira realized she was soaking wet.

Chapter 6

Namur climbed back on to Amira's shoulders, growling in distress. Looking up, Amira saw a boy cradling a half-empty fish bowl that held a rather distressed-looking goldfish.

'It's OK, Semek,' the boy soothed, regarding the glass bowl as if it were a precious jewel.

The goldfish inside, now dangerously low on water, opened and closed its mouth frantically, bubbles floating upwards and popping at the surface. Amira noticed the way its golden scales glistened and shone, like it was made of fire. It was a *jinni*, just like Namur.

She peered at the strange boy through the bowl, which made his head look rather large and his eyes enormous.

'Who are you?' Amira asked, narrowing her eyes.

Namur followed her words with a hiss. Aside from his strange behaviour, the boy was very pale and his hair was the colour of sand. Amira had never seen someone that looked like that before. Everyone she had met at the souk had dark hair and skin, with rich brown eyes to match, just like her. This boy stood out like a shark among dolphins.

She pulled herself to her feet. 'I said,' she repeated, her own bravery surprising her, 'who are you?'

The boy glanced at Amira. 'Sorry,' he said. 'I was just speaking to Semek. He doesn't like souk days, you see. People make him nervous.'

The boy's eyes shifted from Amira to Namur. Amira watched his concern turn to curiosity. 'You have a *jinni*?' he asked suddenly, as if he were accusing Amira of a crime.

He pointed at Namur. Amira swatted his hand away, her frown intensifying. 'So what?' she said. 'Your fish is a *jinni* too.'

The boy peered around, as if he didn't want anyone to see. 'Is it that obvious?' he asked nervously.

'Does it matter?' Amira realized she hadn't really seen any other people with a *jinni*. She hadn't given it much thought before, because she had never really spoken to anyone on land.

The boy sighed. 'Usually I would leave him at home. But he's been acting strange since the storm the other night, and so I thought I would take him to the port to have a dip in the sea.'

'You leave him at home?' Amira gasped. 'Namur and I have never had a day apart,' she added proudly.

The boy frowned at Amira, his head cocked to the side. 'You're not from Failaka, are you?'

Amira blinked. She wasn't sure whether to admit the truth or not, so she scowled.

'I'm sorry if I offended you,' said the boy quickly. 'It's

just you seemed to think having a *jinni* is normal.'

For a brief moment Amira faltered. Was it not? She was too scared to ask. She didn't want the boy to think she was stupid.

'I know it's not normal,' she said defensively.

The boy looked relieved.

'They're only around when people feel angry. Otherwise they're invisible. Most people's *jinn* are invisible,' she said confidently, 'because they don't get angry.'

'Oh, I see.' The boy paused, though he seemed confused about something. 'The thing is, I've never actually met anyone else on this island with a *jinni*,' said the boy. 'You're the first person.'

That surprised Amira. She knew her mothers didn't have *jinn*, but she assumed other people did. Was that why their stall was so busy? Did other people really not have *jinn*? How, then, did they understand emotions?

'And you have to be careful around here,' the boy continued. 'People don't much like magic. Especially *jinn* magic.'

Amira nodded, though she wasn't really listening. 'Are you angry right now?'

'Not really,' said the boy. 'Why?'

'Well, it's just that your *jinni* is visible.'

The boy nodded. 'He appears whenever I'm nervous.'

'Really?' Amira asked, stepping closer. She could smell fresh oranges, though right now there was a bitter edge to them.

'Really,' said the boy earnestly. Then he added, 'Yours appears when you're angry?'

Amira nodded.

'Your anger smells like roses and smoke,' he said, sniffing the air. 'It's getting stronger. You're not going to hurt me, are you?' The boy took a step back, alarmed.

Amira laughed. 'No, of course not! It's just sometimes it feels like a wave of fire washes over me and I say things I don't mean, or just scream as loud as I can. But I don't feel angry right now. Just when you bumped into me.' She wondered, briefly, why Namur was still visible.

The boy nodded understandingly. 'I'm nervous a lot of the time too. It feels similar. But instead of fire, it's water, I think. What are you doing?'

Amira had pulled a pouch of water from her side and poured it into Semek's bowl. 'It's salt water, from the sea.'

The *jinni* swam in circles, as if trying to escape his watery prison. But, as soon as Amira was done, he calmed.

'He likes it,' said Amira smugly, returning her pouch to her pocket.

'Why are you carrying sea water with you?' asked the boy.

'I was feeling landsick, so I thought it would help to have the sea with me.'

'You mean seasick?'

Amira raised her eyebrows. 'No, I mean what I said. *Land*sick.'

'Right,' said the boy, taking a very slight step back. 'I understand.'

Amira could tell from the mixture of smells emanating from him that he didn't understand at all. 'I don't get off the dhow much,' she said rather abruptly.

The boy's face lit up like a freshly stoked fire. 'This whole conversation has been really weird and confusing. But now you've said that I think it all makes sense.'

'OK,' said Amira. Without another word she started off again down the alleyway with the few tonics and cordials that weren't smashed. Amira wanted to prove to her mothers that she was grown-up enough to help at the stall.

Could she lie and tell Dunya that they only had a few more to sell, or would she check the inventory with Jamila and find out Amira had broken some?

'Wait!' The boy jogged over to Amira, his face serious as she turned to meet him. 'Don't you want to know more about all of this? About the *jinn* realm, and the storm?'

'What *jinn* realm?' The tonics were once again pushed to the back of Amira's mind.

'Haven't you ever wondered why you can sense other people's emotions?'

Amira looked into the boy's eyes. She felt the beginnings of something stir, like changing tides.

'I never thought about it,' she admitted. 'My mothers have powers too. I didn't realize there was a *realm*. What does the storm have to do with anything?'

The boy shook his head. 'We need to meet again to talk about this properly. How can I find you?'

'You can stop by my dhow, if you like,' Amira offered, her mind buzzing. Could there be more to having a *jinni* than she first thought? 'It's called *Tigerheart*. It's moored at the port; the dhow with the broken mast and sail.'

'OK,' said the boy. 'I'll stop by later this evening.'

Amira set off again.

'Wait!' the boy called after her.

Amira looked back. 'What now?'

'It's just . . . rude to end a conversation the way you just did.'

Amira shrugged. 'But I had nothing more to say.'

The boy sighed. 'Yes, but when you meet someone new, usually you ask their name, and say it was nice to meet them after.'

Amira was thoughtful for a moment. 'What if it wasn't nice to meet them?'

The boy considered this. 'Then I think you lie.'

'OK,' said Amira. 'What is your name? It was nice to meet you. Was that right?'

The boy laughed. 'I suppose. My name is Leo. What's yours?'

'Amira.' Amira rarely told people her name. She'd never had much of a reason to, and it sounded weird on her tongue. 'Why is your skin so light?' she added.

Leo fell silent.

'Was that rude as well?'

He nodded.

'Sorry,' said Amira. 'It's your eyes too. They look like the sea. Or sapphires. I can't decide.'

Leo grinned, his ears turning pink.

'That wasn't a compliment,' said Amira. 'It's just a fact.'

An awkward silence followed.

'Now I really must go,' Amira said importantly, already walking away. 'I'm very busy at the souk today.'

'Amira?' said Leo after a beat.

She sighed and turned back round to face him again. 'Yes?' she said, trying and failing to sound polite.

'The souk is that way,' he said, pointing in the opposite direction.

'Oh,' said Amira. 'Thank you,' she added, changing course.

'Thank you for the sea water,' Leo called after her. 'I'll see you later!'

Chapter 7

As day turned to night, Amira sat by the port, feet dipped in the sea. Fish darted around her, their movements synchronized. They scattered whenever she wiggled her toes. Her mothers had allowed her to stay out with Namur until the moon rose, as long as they could see her from the cabin window.

She didn't tell them she had planned to meet Leo. She didn't know how to. If he really was the only other person with a *jinni*, what did that mean? He had read Amira's emotions at the souk, but could he do more?

The port was silent, apart from the occasional bleating of Ramady, whose demands increased by the minute. Amira watched as people hurried home before dark, while those who lived on dhows prepared their food, the smell of spiced meat seeping out of their windows.

Tigerheart stood just to Amira's right, with a broken mast, half-ruined deck and shredded sail. It was made from wood the colour of cherries, with a turquoise frame and a golden wheel that glinted in the dying sun. The very end of the bow curved upwards, like a leaping tiger, ready to strike.

To her left, Amira watched a young man collide with a woman carrying a baby. The baby cried out, and the women stumbled, dropping her bag of shopping. The man hurried on, not turning to apologize or check if they were OK. Amira leaped up to help, but the woman had managed to pick herself up and hurry down one of the alleyways before she reached her.

At the souk Amira could smell everyone's emotions so clearly. They were rampant. And yet the people's actions were so different, so lacking. She wasn't used to keeping things buried inside. She just felt what she felt, unquestioningly.

Land people, Amira concluded, were strange.

Namur nuzzled beneath Amira's armpit, dropping something warm and greasy on her lap.

'What's that?' Amira frowned, dropping her voice to a whisper. 'Did you steal this? Namur!'

He looked up at her, his emerald eyes doleful, then

nudged the package with his nose.

Amira cautiously unwrapped the parcel to find a freshly cooked fish inside.

'I suppose it would be a waste not to eat it now,' she reasoned, offering the head and tail to Namur, before taking a big bite from the middle.

They ate together as they watched the sun sink into the horizon. It had been a hot, beautiful day, as if the world was starting anew after the storm. But something was shifting in the sky, and the wind carried with it a hum.

The clouds in the distance – the ones whispered about at the souk – parted, like a curtain, and something revealed itself beyond them.

A giant nest, glowing like fire. And sitting on the nest was a single golden egg, just like the one Amira had stolen for the mermaids long ago. But this egg was moving, coming to life. Lightning struck, and cracks formed at its surface. The shell hatched, piece by piece.

'What *is* that?' asked Amira aloud, discarding the bones of the fish in the ocean and washing her hands in the sea before wiping them on her trousers. She peered at Namur questioningly.

Namur's ears were pulled back. He stood up tall, his fur on end to make him look bigger. He hissed at the horizon, his fangs glinting in the light, and his pupils were nothing but slits.

'Sometimes I wish you could talk, Namur,' Amira said, not taking her eyes off the hatching egg. In the distance it had started to rain. She could tell the sea was choppy by the way the waves lapped at the port. And, judging by the direction of the wind, they would soon find themselves in the midst of another storm.

Amira glanced behind her at the near empty street, searching for a mop of sandy hair.

'I don't think he's coming to meet us,' she said. The disappointment rose to the top of her voice, like a dead fish at sea. Amira was annoyed that Leo had broken his promise. How else would she understand what it meant to have a *jinni* if he wasn't there to share his theories with her?

'Amira!' Dunya suddenly called, her voice shattering the quiet. 'Dinner!'

'Coming!' Amira answered.

She took one last look behind her, but Leo was nowhere to be seen. Amira realized then that she had no way of contacting him. The answers she sought were as lost to her as a leaf swept away by the wind.

As she stepped on to the dhow with Namur wrapped round her shoulders, Amira saw the moon rise, a perfect crescent. She could feel it too, like it was humming in her bones, giving her strength.

Later that night, when her mothers thought she was asleep, Amira heard them whisper in the main cabin. She caught the words 'Namur' and 'truth' and crept to her door, as quietly as she could, to hear more.

'What you did today was dangerous,' Jamila scolded. 'She can't flaunt her powers like that. If they found out . . . You know how they feel about magic on land.'

Dunya scoffed. 'This is the Sahar Peninsula, where magic was born. It's in the very name. You'd think they had all –'

'I think it's time,' said Jamila. 'If she's going to be risking her life, she needs to know.'

'It's too much,' said Dunya with conviction. 'The truth would . . . Well, it would change everything. We need to ease her in. She's only just started her blood cycle . . .

I'll be more careful, I promise,' she added.

Jamila was silent for some time. Amira could hear her sigh. 'Maybe you're right,' she finally replied.

Amira's mothers retreated to their cabin, leaving silence and secrets behind them.

'Did you hear that?' Amira asked, turning to Namur. But he was distracted, perched on the cushion by the windowsill, staring out of her cabin window.

Her mothers, who she shared everything with, were hiding something from her. Something important. Fire flared in her belly, and her anger seeped out of her like smoke.

Amira took her chance. She snuck into the main cabin, with the plan to read the remnants of her mothers' emotions. But when she tried, something blocked her.

Cloves.

Amira scowled.

Her mothers knew cloves weakened her powers. Whatever it was they were hiding, they were doing all they could to stop Amira discovering it.

Which meant she absolutely had to find out the truth, one way or another.

Chapter 8

The next few days at the souk went slowly. Each morning there was sun and clear skies; and each afternoon they were met by cloud and rain.

But the weather wasn't the only thing acting strangely.

Amira was still allowed to come to the souk, but Dunya didn't bring any more tonics or cordials to sell. She asked Amira to knot tapestries instead. Amira knew it had something to do with the conversation she had overheard, and she thought back to the way Leo had acted when he realized she had a *jinni* too.

It was as if everyone was ashamed of magic, as if it was something bad. But that was wrong.

By noon on the third day the storm had returned. The sun disappeared behind a blanket of clouds, plunging the souk into semi-darkness. The energy at the souk shifted. People glanced around nervously, and soon after the first drop of rain fell, they scattered into the alleyways like frightened mice. They weren't used to rain. Not in Failaka, where it was often unbearably hot.

'Have you heard?' one woman declared loudly to her friend. She was standing at the centre of the souk, peering around, obviously wanting to draw attention. 'The port-master's home is gone. The cliff crumbled, like a sandcastle, and plunged into the ocean, taking his house with it. 'It's magic, I tell you!'

A few of the people who had gathered pulled away, shaking their heads. Some chuckled.

'We've all seen the egg, haven't we?' the woman persisted.

The people turned back to her, as if uncertain. They *had* seen it. How could they not? It was standing at the horizon.

'Well?' the woman demanded. 'If it isn't magic, how else do you explain it?'

'An illusion,' a brave teenage boy offered. 'A mirage. My father and I saw one when we travelled through the desert. A great monster, with the head of a wolf and the body of a bird. Our minds can play tricks sometimes . . .'

The woman cackled, holding her arms out as if to

embrace the crowd. 'Are we all seeing it, this mirage, together? How? We aren't starved of food or water.'

Her friend tugged at her sleeve. 'Come on, Umm Abdullah, we should go now. You're causing a scene.'

'So what?' the woman asked loudly. 'Is it better to stay silent than to speak truths? Is it better not to feel than to be fearful? Mark my words. Something is coming for us. And if we choose to hide from it, hold our feelings inside, it'll destroy us all.'

She locked eyes with each member of the crowd, before resting her gaze on Amira. Then she nodded, and allowed herself to be ushered away by her friend. Where she had stood, Amira saw maggots crawling through apple cores that had been left, forgotten, in a wicker basket. The sickly, sweet smell of rotting fruit hung in the air.

When Amira blinked, the basket was gone, as the scent of the woman's fear washed away in the rain.

Chapter 9

'You will act recklessly,' Dunya warned Amira, spreading some cards on the table. 'Tread carefully, and *don't* do anything silly.'

Thunder struck, and lightning followed Dunya's words to illustrate her point. The hens scattered, darting into corners and hiding beneath tables. The group rushed to the window to catch a glimpse of the storm.

The egg had disappeared from the horizon. In its place was a great bird, scuttling around its giant nest.

'It looks like a roc, don't you think?' Amira asked her mothers.

The bird flapped its red wings and a gust of wind sailed overhead. It seemed it could not fly, not yet at least, and it let out a cry of frustration that sounded like thunder.

'Don't be silly,' said Dunya. 'What an imagination you have. It's just the clouds.' But her eyes lingered on the horizon, and Amira knew she was lying.

The sky was dark, the clouds swirling around one another like a whirlpool. It *was* hard to see where the clouds ended and the bird began. But Amira was certain she wasn't seeing things. The bird and its nest were solid.

They had left the souk shortly after the rain had started. Amira had seen, first-hand, the devastation the storm had caused in a few short days. The cliff that had stood overlooking the port was gone, as was the house on top of it. Just as the woman had said.

Wreckage washed to shore from dhows that had been destroyed at sea. Fear had begun to spread like a disease. Amira could see it, like a green snake, slithering from person to person. Rain pitter-pattered against the broken wood of *Tigerheart*, dripping into the cabin. Ramady huffed, making her feelings known.

Leo's words danced through Amira's mind again, and she lingered on the *jinn* realm and the storm. Could they be connected? Could the storm *really* have something to do with *jinn*?

'I think there's more to the storm,' said Amira aloud.

Her mothers glanced at one another, lips pursed.

'What makes you say that?' Jamila asked cautiously.

Amira bit her lip. She didn't want to tell them about Leo. If they were hiding things from her, she could have secrets too. And anyway, she might not ever see him or Semek again.

Dunya let out a strangled laugh. 'There was a woman at the souk today . . .' She told Jamila what had happened.

'Oh, how silly,' said Jamila, waving the story away like it were nothing but a fly. But Amira had read the woman's emotions, and though she didn't understand them, she knew they weren't something to be dismissed. 'The real question is, should we be concerned about this reckless behaviour?' Jamila peered at Amira, face stern. 'What are the cards talking about?'

'I have no idea,' said Amira. 'Why don't *you* tell *me*?' Her words were biting, each one fang-toothed.

Amira had tried, several times, to question her mothers, to pull their secrets out of them. But it was like coaxing pearls from oyster shells. And with each moment they kept silent, Amira could feel her rage building.

Dunya frowned. Amira realized she may have gone a little too far.

'What about my last card?' she said, returning to her cushion, a way to make peace.

Dunya joined her, sitting cross-legged, while Jamila went back to her tonics and cordials.

Rose-scented smoke filled the room, wisps floating around Amira as she listened to her fortune, letting the words wrap round her, protecting her from the storm outside and the uncertainty of her life.

She studied the cards in front of her.

In the first, two mermaids were sitting on a rock in the middle of the ocean, tails intertwined. One mermaid had green hair, like seaweed, and dark skin. The other mermaid was pale, like Leo, and her hair was as red as a blood moon.

The card was called The Lovers. Amira had pulled a face when she saw it, but Dunya explained that the card wasn't always about romantic love. 'It could be the love you have for me and your mother, or Namur.'

The second card was The Fool. It showed a man dressed in a green and blue suit, with a hat covered in feathers. But it wasn't the man's clothes that had struck Amira. It was what he was doing. He hung at the edge of a cliff. Beneath him three sharks circled, waiting for him to fall. This was the card that had preceded Dunya's warning.

Amira hoped her final card would be better. She watched in anticipation as Dunya turned it over.

A dhow, crewed by skeletons, sailed over an ocean red with blood.

Dunya looked up at Amira, her face sombre, as she whispered a single word, 'Death.'

Amira swallowed. 'What does that one mean again?'

As if she needed to ask.

Dunya tried to keep the emotion from her face, but she sounded distressed. 'It means a way of life for you is coming to an end. You'll have new beginnings soon, and things are going to change . . . drastically.' Dunya shared a look with Jamila that Amira couldn't read. She could see the worry seeping from her mothers, like a fog.

'Consider the cards together,' said Dunya. 'Love, recklessness, change.'

Amira wondered if the cards were warning her about her mothers. She had heard them whispering almost every night since the day she first visited the souk, though she could never quite make out what they were saying. All she knew was that they were trying their best to fix the dhow and get away from Failaka as soon as they could.

But why?

Jamila began buzzing around, interrupting Amira's thoughts.

'Put the cards away now please,' she said, her voice clipped. 'Dinner is ready.'

Amira and Dunya made their way to the table where a feast awaited them: spiced rice with dried lime and chicken and a splash of rosewater. They also had fresh salad and fruit, and a whole jug of goat's milk and honey. The hens clucked around them, unaware that one of their own was about to be devoured at the table. Ramady lifted her head and sniffed at the food, but she didn't seem to feel it worth scavenging.

'The animals need to go outside soon,' Jamila observed. 'They're taking up far too much room.'

Namur took his place round Amira's neck, and she fed him pieces of chicken while she served her food. Every few moments he would nudge her arm with his paw to tell her he wanted more.

'I have a new tonic I need you both to test before we begin,' Jamila continued.

'What is it this time?' asked Dunya, piling rice on to her plate.

'To ease the worries that come before an important encounter.'

'You might need to work on the description,' Dunya teased, squeezing Jamila's hand affectionately. She smelled the mixture and took a tentative sip. 'It's very refreshing.'

Jamila's anxious face eased a little. 'Oh, good. Can you

tell what ingredients I used?'

Dunya tasted again. 'Mint. And a botanical, but I couldn't tell you which.'

Jamila smiled. 'And?'

As the pair of them discussed ingredients, Amira felt Jamila's mixture work its way down her throat, filling her with warmth. It spread from her belly to every part of her body, until it was as if fire might shoot out of her fingers.

Finally, she felt brave enough to ask questions that would lead her to the truth.

'Do you know anything about other *jinn*?' blurted Amira.

Her mothers were quiet for a beat too long.

'No, my darling,' said Dunya, clearing her throat. 'Why do you ask?' Her lies came in waves of garlic and seaweed, the smell of them swimming down Amira's throat.

'I heard some kids talking about *jinn* at the souk the other day.'

'Sounds fascinating,' said Jamila in a bad attempt at earnestness. 'Why don't we take a moment to raise a glass?'

'To what?' Amira asked, an edge to her voice.

'To starting your blood cycle,' said Dunya.

'And a successful week at the souk,' added Jamila.

Something sharp stirred in Amira's belly, like nails. Her mothers knew more about *jinn*, but they were keeping it from her. Why? And what else were they hiding?

Amira felt the carefully knotted tapestry of her life begin to unravel piece by piece. She longed to return to sea, where all she had worried about was which direction the wind was going.

Then, like an unexpected wave taking them off course, there was a knocking at the door.

Chapter 10

'I'll get it,' Dunya offered, standing up from the table.

When Amira saw who it was, she choked on her milk.

Leo entered the room, his face lighting up when he spotted her. The rain hadn't stopped since the afternoon, and he was soaking wet, his hair dripping on to his shoulders.

Leo!' Amira spluttered, standing up awkwardly.

Jamila raised her eyebrows at Amira. 'The boy has a name?'

'Of course he has a name,' muttered Amira.

'And why are you familiar with it?' Jamila put both hands on her hips.

'Come inside and get dry,' Dunya interrupted loudly, drowning out Jamila's clipped responses. 'It's very wet out this evening, isn't it?' she said, as if rain in the middle of summer, on the outskirts of the desert, was a normal occurrence.

'Thank you,' Leo replied. 'Hello, Amira.'

He waved at Amira awkwardly from across the room, Semek and his bowl tucked under his other arm. Amira wanted to move towards him, but it was as if she was stuck in quicksand.

'Amira, why didn't you tell us you made a friend?' Dunya was smiling, but her narrowed eyes told a different story. She kept glancing at Semek, as did Jamila.

'Well . . .' Amira began, with no idea of how to continue. Jamila's eyebrows had crawled so far up her forehead they threatened to join her hairline.

Namur jogged up to Leo and stood on his hind legs, placing both paws on Leo's knees in what looked to be a greeting. He was visible again. It seemed to be his usual form these days. But neither Amira nor her mothers noticed the exchange, as they were whispering furiously to one another in the corner.

'Why didn't you tell us you had made a *friend*?' asked Jamila.

'Maybe I'm not the only one who has secrets,' Amira spat, her words hissing and fizzing like boiling water.

'What exactly does that mean?' Jamila raised her voice

loud enough for Leo to hear in the cramped quarters of the dhow.

Namur returned to Amira now, rubbing his body over her legs, as if he knew the feel of his soft fur would comfort her. She absent-mindedly crouched down to stroke him, and he pushed his face into her palm and licked her wrist.

'It's clear we're all getting a bit worked up,' Dunya said. 'Let's take a moment to express how we're feeling, shall we?'

Amira and Jamila glared at one another.

Dunya sighed.

'Fine,' said Jamila, crossing her arms. 'I'll go first. You were supposed to be watching her, Dunya!' she began. It was the first time Amira had seen her mothers properly snap at one another. 'And instead you let her show off her magic, *and* go off and meet a boy?'

'I apologized for the situation in the souk the other day, and I didn't let her *go off and meet a boy*,' said Dunya, wounded. 'I – Well . . .' She blinked furiously, as if holding back tears.

Jamila frowned, and Amira could see the anger fade from her eyes. 'It's OK,' she said, patting her wife's arm.

'It's just when did – Hello, Leo!' She showed her teeth in what wasn't quite a smile. 'You crept up behind us very quietly. Impressive!'

'Sorry,' Leo said, his ears glowing red. 'I wanted to invite Amira over to my house for dinner, if that's all right?'

'Amira's already eaten,' said Jamila bluntly.

Dunya pursed her lips but said nothing.

'Oh.' Leo laughed, awkwardly. 'How about tomorrow?'

'I'd love to come over tomorrow, Leo,' Amira said at once.

The room fell silent. Even Ramady didn't stir.

'Is there a reason I can't go?' Amira turned to her mothers, challenging them. If they said no, they would be forced to explain why.

'I . . .' Jamila began. 'Well . . .'

The goat bleated from her corner in response.

Chapter 11

By the next day the rain had stopped. In its place was a fierce wind, bringing with it a strange buzzing in the air, like a hive of bees. Amira could feel it on her skin; it made the hairs on her arms stand on end.

Dunya and Amira didn't attend the souk. Instead, they focused on fixing the dhow, with the plan to leave before the moon was full again.

Namur was even more distressed, pacing around the perimeter of the cabin, careful to avoid Ramady's fort in the corner. Amira still didn't understand why he was constantly there - visible. She didn't feel particularly angry at the moment, just out of sorts.

The chickens had insisted on staying inside, curled up in the strangest places. All day, as Amira carried out her chores, she would find them beneath her bedcovers, or wedged between a cushion and the cabin wall. When one chicken landed on Amira's head, feathers cascading everywhere, Jamila finally banished them to the deck.

Though Amira was under strict instructions not to leave the dhow (not that her mothers had explained why), she stole glances outside the cabin windows and read the emotions of those who passed by on the port.

It was as if the great big snake of fear had grown to the width of a tree and wrapped round them all, squeezing their feelings inside until they all suffocated.

None of them looked towards the ocean, at the great bird in its nest. They simply scuttled, heads down, from one place to the next. But they were afraid. Amira heard, through the open window of her room, whispers of curses. The port was emptier, some people choosing to stay indoors, hiding inside their homes, shrinking into themselves like turtles in their shells.

It seemed only the woman at the souk was willing to face the truth. The woman – and Amira and Leo.

Later that evening the clouds were red and bright across the turquoise sky, like an open wound, as Amira met Leo at the empty port. Dunya and Jamila had reluctantly agreed to let her visit him, but only for an hour, and she had impatiently counted down the minutes until she would finally find out more about *jinn*.

The stormbird, as Amira now called it, was bigger now. Every so often it let out a roar, like thunder, followed by lightning.

She was surprised at how quickly she had become used to its presence. Once all she had seen was the horizon, waiting to be discovered. Now her eyes were drawn to the monster in the distance. She was used to the sound too, the tuneless anger of the wind as it howled into the night. But both storm and horizon disappeared from sight as the pair and their *jinn* launched themselves into a narrow alleyway Amira had not walked down before.

'I'm sorry about my mothers,' she said. 'They were rude to you last night.'

Amira watched Leo's lips turn upwards as he replied, 'I like them.'

'You do?' Amira was surprised. Jamila had been practically hostile!

'They care about you. So much.'

Leo's voice changed as he spoke. It was heavy, as if covered in armour and loaded with weapons, ready to fight. But Amira was too busy with her own worries to notice. Something had landed hard in her belly, like an anchor dropped from a great height.

If they care so much, why are they hiding things from me?

Amira thought of the odd expression on Jamila's face after Leo had left the night before. Try as she might, she hadn't been able to read her mother's emotions. Jamila had used so many spices in her tonics that Amira's eyes had streamed, and all she could smell was cloves.

When Amira had shut the cabin door behind her to meet Leo that evening, she'd heard her mothers' hushed whispers. And she knew there was a story there, a story they had chosen not to share with her, though stories were what they had shared their whole lives.

But now Amira had other ways of finding out answers. She had Leo.

They approached a modest house, sandwiched between several others like books on a shelf. Amira followed Leo inside, Namur asleep on her shoulders. She could feel her *jinni*'s mouth twitching, his whiskers tickling her neck. Every few moments he let out a very quiet growl, and his fur stood on end, the way it did when he felt threatened.

She realized he was having a nightmare.

When Namur was a kitten, he'd had nightmares often. They would wake Amira just as the moon was at its highest, and she would cradle him close until his whimpers ceased and his breathing returned to normal.

Tonight Amira made sure to stroke his tail every few moments so he felt her presence.

She wished she understood why he seemed so afraid. She knew, somehow, that it was to do with the bird, and the storm.

Amira had tried not to get angry over the last couple of days so Namur could stay in his pure invisible form, where he was more powerful. But it hadn't seemed to work. Something about the storm was keeping him here; she just couldn't understand what.

The main hall of Leo's house was small and cramped, furniture squeezed into every corner. Amira faced a set of stairs that wound up into the ceiling. A single door stood to her right. It led to a room that reminded Amira a little of the main cabin on the dhow, with a table at the centre and walls filled with cooking supplies.

Through the open door floated a beautiful voice,

though it sounded muffled, as if someone had wrapped a piece of cloth round the singer's mouth.

'Is that your mum?' asked Amira. 'Her voice is beautiful!'

'Come inside,' said Leo, ignoring her question.

Amira followed him through to the kitchen, where the sound grew louder. But no one was inside. At the stove was a steaming pot, its contents bubbling, spilling on to the counter beneath it. It sizzled and hissed. Leo rushed towards it, cursing.

'Where's that music coming from?' asked Amira, trying to find the source of the singing. Her voice rose in panic. 'Is this house haunted?'

She followed the voice around the room until she found a small red box with black dials on it. She put her ear to the box and listened. The voice continued to sing, clearer now.

'Have you trapped a ghoul inside?' Amira asked, fascinated. 'How did you catch it?'

'Of course not,' Leo said. 'It's a radio. Have you never seen one before?'

Amira shook her head.

'It's a box that plays music. Look . . .'

He turned the dial in one direction and the sound disappeared entirely. Amira gasped. Then he turned the dial the other way and it grew louder and louder, until it filled the room again, like birdsong in the morning.

'A music box?'

'Yes! Exactly.'

Amira fiddled with the dials, enjoying the way the sound changed. Leo even showed her how to tune it so it played different songs.

'It's like magic!' Amira declared, and Leo laughed.

'It's science actually,' he explained. 'Hang on, I just need to get something from upstairs. I'll be back in a minute.'

Leo's kitchen was much neater than the one on the dhow. Pots lined up like soldiers, and books had been put away neatly on shelves. Amira tried to read the spines of a few, but they used words she didn't recognize: words like 'chemistry' and 'physics'.

On a table next to the shelf of books, just behind the radio, was a framed drawing of a woman with red hair and a man that looked a little bit like Leo. They were cradling a small boy, who couldn't have been much older than three.

Amira picked up the drawing, marvelling at how real it looked.

'Don't touch that!'

Leo startled Amira, waking Namur up. She hadn't heard him come back into the room. He snatched up the drawing – he was wearing gloves now, she noticed – and placed it in a drawer by the fire. Namur leaped off Amira's shoulder and promptly began to sniff around.

'I –' Amira began, but Leo interrupted her.

'Why don't you sit down?' he said. His smile looked as plastered on as Jamila's the night before.

Amira watched him closely as he served their food. 'Why are you wearing gloves?' she asked.

'It's hard to explain,' said Leo, his voice pained.

'What's science?' Amira asked instead, thinking about the way he had described the radio. She assumed it must be a branch of magic. She could see Leo's shoulders drop as he relaxed a little at the question.

'Well . . .' he began, and he told her all about radios and other inventions while they each helped themselves to some some food.

'I don't understand it!' Amira said sometime later, after Leo had tried to explain electricity and switches to her. 'You can't just poke things to make them work.' Frustration dripped from her words as she irritably picked at the food on her plate.

'How do you explain the lights in this room, then?' Leo countered.

'Fire,' said Amira simply.

Leo laughed. 'Have you never been to school?'

Amira scowled at Leo. She knew *school* very well. It was the name for a group of fish. But she had no idea what that had to do with fireballs trapped in glass.

Amira knew she was bad at learning about new things. If she didn't understand something, she would ignore it, and pretend it didn't exist. But she was quickly discovering that life on land was different; there was much more to it than she first thought. Still, Leo was acting like a such a know-it-all, and he hadn't even told her anything important yet.

'Enough about science,' said Amira, waving a hand the way Jamila did when she wanted to move the conversation on. 'What about the storm, and the *jinn* realm?'

Leo put his knife and fork down, and looked up at Amira, his face serious.

'Well, I don't know much,' he began. 'It's just a . . . well, a theory. We can read emotions through our senses, can't we?'

Amira nodded.

'And that's because of our *jinn*.'

Amira frowned. She already knew this.

'But when they're invisible, they leave behind a *current*,

don't they?'

'Like the sea?' asked Amira.

'Sort of. But in the air instead.'

Amira nodded again. She had felt the current. It was like a buzzing whenever Namur was invisible but still sitting on her shoulders.

'Well, in science, everything has to come from somewhere. And it has to *go* somewhere too. That means our *jinn* must be going somewhere when they turn invisible, and that's where all of the emotions we're reading are stored. We connect the *jinn* to the human realm. Without us they would be invisible forever, and all the emotions would be buried deep . . .'

Amira's head was swirling like a tornado, but she could understand what Leo was explaining. Whenever she read emotions she could smell them, or see them, or just *feel* them. It was like another layer to her world, one no one else could access. Not even her mothers.

'But what does that have to do with the storm?' Amira finally asked.

'Well,' said Leo, 'I've been testing out equipment to sense the energy in –'

Amira put her hand up to stop him. 'No more science.'

'Uh . . .' Leo spluttered, his ears turning pink. He hopped up from his chair. 'It might be easier to just show you.'

He ran to one of the cupboards in the kitchen, and rummaged through a bag, finally pulling out a metal sphere. Then he walked over to Amira and held the sphere out.

'Touch it,' he said.

Amira looked up at him, frowning. 'Why?'

'If you want to know more about the stormbird, this will explain it.'

Amira placed a tentative finger on the metal sphere. She immediately felt a zap.

'Ouch!' she said, pulling back.

But for some reason she wanted to try again. She put her whole hand round the sphere this time, and felt a jolt through her bones. 'Wow,' she said, peering at it. 'What is it?'

'The current we were talking about, the current that surrounds our *jinn* when they're invisible,' said Leo. 'This sphere captures it. It all started the night the storm arrived.

You might not have felt it right away, but it's getting stronger. It's why Semek is acting strange.'

'Namur too,' said Amira, turning to her *jinni*. He was pacing around Leo's kitchen, the way he had in the cabin. 'So this is coming from the stormbird, just like the current our *jinn* leave behind when they're invisible?'

'Well done!' said Leo, which Amira thought was a bit patronising.

She rolled her eyes at him. 'I'm not stupid,' she snapped. 'But why is the stormbird giving off the current when it's visible? And does this mean the stormbird is a *jinni*? Where is its human?'

'I don't know,' admitted Leo. 'Maybe some *jinn* don't need humans, or turn invisible at all.'

Amira made sure to remember everything Leo had told her so she could thread all of this new information together later, the way she collected rope and knotted her tapestries.

'We'll figure it out,' she said, while Leo cleared their plates, leaving only the metal sphere on the table, gently humming. Then she asked a question that had been playing on her mind since she first arrived.

'Why did you hide that drawing of your parents?' she asked. Leo's back was turned, but even so she could see him stiffen. 'It's a photograph,' he muttered. When Amira asked him what that word meant he didn't respond.

'Leo?' Amira persisted.

He put the plates down and turned round. His face was scrunched up in an expression she hadn't seen him wear before. Leo's emotions were usually as fresh as oranges, but right now they were sickly, like fruit turning sour.

'Sometimes, Amira, you need to learn when to mind your own business.'

The venom in his voice surprised her. Amira wasn't used to being snapped at, so she responded as a cat would: by hissing louder.

'Why do you keep wearing your gloves? And why are you mad right now? And why –'

'I didn't realize you came round to spy on me,' interrupted Leo. 'I thought you wanted to know more about the storm and the *jinn* realm.'

'I do,' Amira began, 'but –'

'Then let's talk about THAT!' spat Leo.

'Fine!'

Amira was now too riled by Leo's rudeness to gather her thoughts. Namur, who had given up his pacing in the midst of their argument, launched himself at Semek's bowl.

'AND GET YOUR STUPID CAT AWAY FROM MY FISH,' exploded Leo, grabbing Namur and throwing him to the floor.

'Don't touch my *jinni!*' yelled Amira. Namur returned to her shoulders, hissing at Leo. 'Don't you DARE touch Namur again!'

Amira and Leo were standing now, facing one another like two dhows going into battle. A knock on the door interrupted them.

'That'll be your mother,' said Leo, breathless with anger. 'I think you should leave.'

There was another knock.

Leo turned the radio on and started washing the pans at the sink, as if she'd already left. Amira was furious. *He* was the one who had asked her round.

'Leo!' she shouted over the sound of the radio.

Leo said nothing. Somehow the silence was worse than him yelling at her.

'Leo!' Amira tried again, softening her voice.

Leo turned slowly, his hands wet and covered in soap. 'Get out,' he said.

Amira opened her mouth to retort, but then she closed it again. If he didn't want to be her friend any more, she wasn't going to try to change his mind.

The person at the door knocked for the third time.

'Finally!' Dunya said, when Amira answered. 'Shall we stay for a little while? Or are you finished?'

'I'm done,' Amira said darkly, scowling towards Leo. 'Let's go.'

'OK,' Dunya said, raising an eyebrow. 'A little intense at the moment, aren't we?'

Amira, Namur and Dunya walked home in silence, each in their own world.

If she no longer had Leo to figure out the truth about the stormbird, Amira thought, she would just have to get the answers herself.

Tonight.

Chapter 12

Amira's cabin was cramped, with a wooden bed bolted to the floor next to a round window. By her bed were a stack of books she read before going to sleep – stories filled with beanstalks and secret gardens in lands unfamiliar – and a pile of clothes messily stuffed into a corner.

But, she realized, she had no books about *her* world. The Sahar Peninsula and the *jinn* realm. The world she navigated every day. Amira trawled through them all, flicking pages angrily, tearing a few in her haste to find out something, anything, about *jinn*.

She had always known that was what Namur was. It was something her mothers had taught her when she was young, just as they all shared stories about other magic in the world. But she had never known, until she visited the souk, that magic was something to keep hidden.

After hours of searching, Amira had learned nothing. Her mothers had long gone to bed, and Namur was curled up on her pillow, waiting for her to settle.

Amira threw the last book – a story about a witch who uses her flying skills to deliver packages – at the wall, stomped around for a bit, and let the thoughts swirl through her mind.

The stormbird was visible. That much was clear. So if Namur appeared whenever Amira was angry, and Semek appeared when Leo was nervous, then what emotion was causing the stormbird to appear? And if it didn't have a human, then how was it visible at all? And why was it so big?

It had something to do with the *jinn* realm. Amira just *knew* it. But what?

Outside Amira's small, round window stood a rowing boat, rocking gently in the waves. Beyond the boat was the remnants of the port-master's house, which had collapsed into the ocean.

And beyond all of that was the stormbird.

How could they stop the stormbird? And if they didn't stop it, would it destroy all of Failaka and the rest of the Sahar Peninsula?

Amira realized, in that moment, that not all answers

are written in books. Sometimes we have to write them ourselves. She grabbed her jacket and boots and turned to Namur.

'Come on,' she said. 'We're going fishing for answers.'

Chapter 13

Waves lapped up against the side of the dhow as Amira and Namur snuck out of her room. In the distance the stormbird cried out. It was growing and seemed more and more restless as it did. Amira wondered what would happen when it grew big enough to fly. Would it leave the nest? What then?

Amira had to pass by her mothers' door to get outside, and she crept carefully, avoiding the floorboards she knew would creak. The barometer spun and clattered, the sound masking Amira's steps. Her mothers' gentle snores followed her all the way up to the deck, where the wind was blowing fiercely.

The stormbird cried again as Amira climbed down to the port. The storm had weakened, the cracking thunder had stopped, and the rain had abated. But the water was choppy, reaching for the dhow as if trying to pull it under.

Amira wound round to the back of the dhow, where

her mothers wouldn't see her, and climbed into the rowing boat. Namur curled round her neck like a scarf, his body shaking. He growled as she untied the boat from their dhow.

'I know,' said Amira. Though Namur didn't speak words, she understood what he was trying to say to her. *You're being reckless. Stupid.* Like her tarot cards had warned.

Amira knew Namur as well as she knew herself. Namur hated having his belly rubbed and he despised human feet. Fish was his favourite food, though he also loved rice. And he never, *ever* liked to be held. He *chose* to sit on Amira's shoulders, not the other way around.

'I have to find out what all of this means, Namur.'

And, with nowhere else to turn, Amira turned to the sea for answers.

Namur grumbled again, though more softly.

'It's not my fault,' Amira snapped. 'My mothers won't speak to me, and Leo . . .' She pushed any thought of Leo to the back of her mind. If he didn't want to be friends with her, that was fine. Though, deep down, she knew it wasn't. But she had decided to lie to herself, like the people on land.

Namur was silent then, and she knew he understood the importance of their mission. He was a *jinni*, after all. And the stormbird was connected to his world.

The half-moon waved at her, and Amira waved back before she started rowing. She always felt just a little bit braver whenever the moon watched over her. It was as if she gathered her strength from it in the way of the tides. And tonight she needed all the strength she could get as she drove herself and her *jinni* into the storm.

Amira rowed slow and steady, with Namur still clinging to her shoulders, while rain lashed her face. She could feel his claws dig in, and it hurt, but she didn't tell him. The truth was, she was just as afraid.

But she was angry too, at Leo, her mothers. And she let that anger fuel her. She let it hum from her chest to her arms and into the oars, as she powered the boat forward.

The sky was covered in a grey blanket of clouds. It wasn't raining, so Amira could see the path ahead clearly, but the waves picked up the further she rowed from the shore. Soon they were twice her height, rolling towards her, and she had to concentrate, riding over them, so the boat didn't topple.

The sea foamed as the waves broke, leaving strands of white behind, like veins on a giant hand. The waves were pulling her back, away from the stormbird. It was as if the ocean wanted to drag Amira and Namur back to shore.

But Amira sailed on.

Behind her, Failaka shrank into the darkness, and ahead the storm shone bright beneath the moon.

A shadowy tail darted beneath the surface. Then two, then three.

It couldn't be. Could it?

She saw a glimpse again. Blue, green and purple. It couldn't be . . . Not here.

Mermaids.

Amira didn't have time to think. The waves were getting fiercer. She started to lose control of the boat. She could feel the waves crash into it, the wood creaking. Then, something pulled at the oars.

Amira grabbed hold of them with all of her strength, growling with the effort. But the sea was stronger. It snatched one of the oars away, cracking the rowlock. She quickly pulled the second oar up and placed it safely in the boat.

'Hold on tight, Namur,' Amira said.

She used her bodyweight to steer the boat now, leaning left and right into the waves as she inched closer and closer to the storm.

After the third wave crashed over them, leaving Amira and Namur soaking wet, something in the air shifted.

'Can you feel that, Namur?' Amira yelled over the sound of the waves.

Namur let out a strangled cry, whiskers buried into her neck. She wished she didn't have to put him through this. But then, he was her *jinni*, and they did everything together.

The air was fizzing with energy. Amira could feel it vibrate in her bones.

But no matter how much Amira steered, she couldn't seem to get closer to the stormbird's nest. Even as the water grew choppier and the current in the air stronger.

The stormbird's body was golden at its core, fading to yellow, then orange, then red at its outer edges. It was like a flame made of feathers. The bird was the size of *Tigerheart*, big enough to crush human bones, and so bright Amira could barely look at it. But it was looking right at Amira and Namur with eyes like stars. It snapped its hooked beak once, then twice, and flexed its great talons.

It can't fly, Amira reminded herself. *It can't fly . . . Yet.*

The stormbird flapped its giant wings, sending a whoosh of wind so powerful that sea spray whipped Amira's face, stinging her cheeks. It rose a little before letting out a roar of frustration that sounded like thunder. It flapped its wings again, rising higher.

Namur clung to Amira's shoulders, hissing violently.

'It's OK,' she said, stroking his sopping fur. But it wasn't. They had one oar and no way of rowing against the waves. They were trapped, their boat swaying in circles beneath the stars.

The third time the stormbird flapped its wings, it stayed in the air.

It could fly. Dread coursed through Amira. Had it just learned how?

And then, like a bolt of lightning, the stormbird shot straight for Amira and Namur.

Amira didn't think. She just acted.

She launched herself into the ocean, letting herself be taken by the waves like a leaf in the breeze. She swirled

and twirled beneath the waves and tried to keep her eyes on the surface. The bright red of the stormbird hovered above her, threatening to snatch her from the sea.

When Amira broke the surface to gasp a breath, she realized Namur was no longer on her shoulders.

'Namur?' she cried, whipping her head round.

She spotted the boat. It had overturned, and Namur was clinging to its hull, crying out for her.

'Namur!' Amira said, waving. 'I'm here.' He saw her and let out another cry. 'It's OK, Namur, I'm coming!'

She desperately tried to swim towards her *jinni*, but the waves pulled her away as the stormbird circled the upturned rowing boat.

Amira felt a chill seep into her bones, like ice. *No!* She was furious with herself for putting Namur in danger.

That's when she knew what she had to do. *Stop feeling angry. Stop feeling angry. Stop feeling angry.* Amira repeated the words over and over in her head. If she could just calm herself, surely Namur would turn invisible and then the stormbird wouldn't harm him?

But the thing about emotions is that they're not flies that buzz around us to be swatted. They're roots. They're a part of us, growing and flourishing as we nurture them. And sometimes we can't escape them, no matter how hard we try.

'Swim!' Amira screamed over the sound of crashing waves. 'Namur, swim!'

Namur's fur was so wet and flattened that he looked like a kitten. He paused – and he jumped.

As Namur leaped, the stormbird dived.

Its talons clasped Namur's tiny body, caging him in its claws.

'No!' Amira screamed. The pain in her chest felt as if the stormbird had pierced through her heart. 'Let him go!'

A wave broke over her and she struggled back to the surface again.

When she next looked, the stormbird had returned to its nest.

Something grabbed hold of Amira, pulling her beneath the surface of the water. Her vision blurred. All she could see were two tails, blue and purple, circling her like a halo. Above the water the stars winked, and the moon waved.

And, after that, everything turned dark.

Chapter 14

Hello again. Did you forget about me? Who, then, did you think was telling you this story? I'll forgive you, I suppose. Just this once.

Shall we get back to the matter at hand?

All stories have beginnings, as I explained. But they have middles too. This, right here, is the middle of our story. Usually this is where things start to go a little badly, as is the case with Amira.

Where has the stormbird taken Namur? And why?

And is Amira OK?

We can't be certain what might happen, because stories don't always have happy endings.

I shan't say any more. Not yet, anyway. Because I'm afraid our friends have several more obstacles to face. And you must be patient and face them too, before you know the outcome.

Oh, all right. I'll give you one hint. Just one.

Do you remember the story Amira told? About the mermaids?

Well, we're about to see what happens next . . .

There will be other stories, as we continue. Pay close attention. Because in the heart of these stories lie the answers you're searching for, the answers Amira's searching for – if she could just pay attention for long enough to find them.

Will you pay attention? Will you find the answers for her?

I'll help you along: Amira was right about the stormbird. It is a *jinni* of sorts, but there's a little more to it than that. And she was very clever to notice that it has a current even though it is always visible. But why? And how can she stop it?

Now, we really must carry on with our story. I don't have much time left with which to tell it. I only have until the full moon.

So forgive me if I speed things up a little . . .

Chapter 15

Amira woke up clutching her hands to her neck. Her breaths came in long, desperate gasps. She peered around and waited for her eyes to adjust.

She was damp, hair sopping wet, lying on the bleached dock of Failaka port. The sun was just beginning to rise, and the first bleary-eyed workers were leaving their houses. A few turned to look at Amira, but no one came to help.

She pulled herself up, confused. Had she fallen asleep outside? And where was Namur? She couldn't feel him . . .

When the realisation hit her, it was as if she had been dunked into the ice-cold ocean once more. Her entire body went numb, and her brain froze. But it was more than that. It was a feeling that couldn't be grasped, like grains of sand slipping from your palm.

Have you ever accidentally put on two different shoes? Or slept somewhere new and woke up wondering where you are? This felt a little bit like that. Except the feeling came from Amira's skin and bones. It was as if she were living someone else's life, and she wanted to shed herself of it and crawl back to Namur.

But she couldn't, because he was gone.

The waves turned calm, and the clouds cleared. In the distance the stormbird was asleep in its nest. It seemed peaceful, as if it hadn't just turned Amira's world upside down. Was Namur in its nest, too? But if it was at the horizon, how would she get there?

After a moment of frozen panic, Amira began to cry. Gently at first, like the beginnings of a sad song, but building slowly up into a crescendo, the sobs taking hold of her body.

Amira retched into the ocean like she had that very first day she stepped on land. But this time Namur wasn't there to comfort her. She couldn't feel his whiskers tickle her skin, or his soft purrs. And she didn't know if she had the strength to pick herself back up.

Eventually – it might have been hours, or it might have been minutes – Amira dragged herself to her room while her mothers were still asleep, and sank deep, deep, deep into her bed.

'Amira!' Jamila called, slamming her door open. 'Wake up, we fixed the dh— What's wrong? What happened to you? What . . . Dunya!' She called for her wife, panicked. 'Dunya!'

Amira was curled up into a ball on her bed, with the remnants of the sea around her. Seaweed clung to her feet and grazes lined her legs from where she had scraped them against rocks in the ocean. Her eyes were puffy from crying, and she felt as if a great weight was holding her down. She couldn't move, couldn't speak.

Dunya came in. Her mothers pulled Amira up and checked her over.

'What happened? Are you hurt? Talk to us!' Jamila was crying too.

Dunya put a hand on her wife's arm. 'Give her a moment,' she said patiently, though her own voice was shaking. 'She'll tell us when she's ready.'

Jamila rushed out of the room. Dimly, Amira could hear her mother mixing something in the main cabin. Everything sounded strange, as if Amira were still under water, watching the world from a distance. It didn't feel as if she were part of it any more.

'Drink up,' said Jamila, rushing back inside Amira's cabin. She offered Amira a cup of tea mixed with a golden liquid that smelled like oranges. It reminded her of Leo.

At first Amira didn't move.

'Drink it,' said Jamila again, her hands shaking. 'Please,' she whispered.

Dunya helped Amira up and placed pillows behind her back for support. Slowly, Amira sipped her tea. She felt the liquid swim down her throat into her belly. It was as if she had been frozen for a thousand years.

The liquid woke Amira, but it numbed her too. Perhaps that was best. She didn't want to be angry any more. What good did it do? It had driven her away from her mothers, and Leo. It was her anger that had caused Namur to be snatched away. She had rowed them out to sea because she was angry, and because of that Namur couldn't turn invisible when the stormbird found them.

Amira drank the tea, and then she asked for more.

When Jamila returned the second time, Amira spoke.

'Namur,' she said, cradling his name on her tongue. 'Namur is gone.'

And it's all my fault.

As the words left her lips, Amira felt as if all of her senses had disappeared. The sounds of birds had ceased to exist, and all of the colours were faded. Her world was crumbling like a sand sculpture in the wind.

She told her mothers everything.

She told them about what Leo had revealed, the conversations she heard her mothers have at night. And she told them about the stormbird – how she had travelled to find answers, and how it had snatched Namur from the upturned boat.

When she was finished, Amira started crying again. So did her mothers. Jamila took the mug from Amira's hands and placed it by her bedside. Dunya brought a tub of warm water and a clean cloth, and bathed Amira right there in her bed. Then, silently, she dressed Amira in dry, clean clothes.

'We'll find him,' said Jamila. 'I'm sure of it.'

'I'm so sorry we dismissed you when you tried to talk to us about the stormbird,' said Dunya passionately. 'We were so worried about . . . We were wrong. And I am so sorry for that. Truly. But from now on, I will listen, and I won't leave your side.' She caressed Amira's hair as she lay next to her. 'Not as long as you need me.'

At the end of the bed Jamila's eyes were distant, red raw from crying. 'It's true that we have been keeping secrets,' she said. 'And I think it's time we told you the truth.'

Jamila left the room and returned with the bakhoor pot. A single piece of coal lay inside it, glowing red hot. On to the coal, she dropped perfumed wood chips that smelled like the sea. She danced around the room, the smoke following her movements like a charmed snake.

The smoke took shape. Waves rolling beneath a dhow, much smaller than *Tigerheart*. And at its helm stood two sea witches looking towards the horizon.

The Fifth Voyage of Dunya and Jamila, the Sea Witches

Two young sea witches set off on their fifth voyage. They had fought ghouls and dined with desert dwellers. They had even conversed with mermaids. They had glimpsed mountains of ice, and deserts of fire, but they had never before seen a city of brass.

One day, the first sea witch was adjusting the sail on their dhow, when she saw something glint from the water below.

Was it a pearl? Or, perhaps, just a trick of the sun.

The first sea witch called to the second, who was steering the dhow towards the wind, and their eyes fell on several more objects sparkling from the deep. Then the first sea witch, the stronger swimmer, dived into the water to inspect their findings.

She had been under for almost a minute, and the second sea witch was beginning to worry. But as she was about to join her wife, she saw a hand burst out of the water, holding a bottle made of brass.

The second sea witch leaned forward and helped the first out of the water. She took the bottle and studied it.

'Where did it come from?' she asked.

Upon closer inspection the brass was solid, with a pearl acting as its lid. A single bottle alone would pay for food for a year.

'I don't know,' the first answered, drying herself off in the sun. 'But I see some more of them in the sea!'

'Let's collect them all!' the second sea witch said, her eyes sparkling like the bottle in her hands.

Now, the sea witches were used to hunger, living from dry stores on their dhow for weeks. They went months on their voyages without glimpsing land. And often, when they stumbled across an island, they barely had a handful of coins to trade for fresh food.

The discovery they made that day on the dhow was life-changing, but not in the way they had first anticipated.

The sea witches searched, day and night, for more bottles. They searched until the moon rose full and red on the third night.

As the first sea witch rescued her eighth bottle from the ocean, she saw, in front of her, a glittering island that looked like a treasure box. And they decided to explore it, to embark on their next adventure.

It was dark when the sea witches reached the shore, and so we must forgive their mistakes on that fateful night.

At the very centre of the island stood a beautiful palace made of brass. The walls shimmered in the moonlight. But a red haze surrounded everything, as if it had been drenched in blood.

The blood moon shone bright and full, and the sea witches knew to be careful around magic at such a time. It was strongest when the moon was full, but that meant it could be unpredictable too.

Surrounding the palace were buildings of brass, their doors and windows made of brass too. They were as tall as trees, and as wide as dhows, and positioned as neatly as worker ants. The buildings spread outwards from the palace, protecting it like soldiers.

'Look,' the second sea witch said to the first, pointing into the middle distance. 'A horse! And a man.'

The sea witches approached with caution, as experience had taught them. They did not know whether the people on this island would be friendly. They suspected the man and his horse were patrolling for intruders, just like them.

But, when the sea witches stepped closer, they found the man and his horse were not real at all, but statues made of brass.

'Come, look!' the first sea witch said. The statue, if melted down, would buy them a new dhow. A bigger one. But how would they lift it? 'We can take the man's helmet, and his sword. Then his boots and his armour. Piece by piece, we can carry the statue to the dhow.' She reached out, her eyes hungry for all she could buy, but the second sea witch stopped her.

'Be careful,' she said. 'We don't know this place. Let's look around first.'

The first sea witch did not agree. Why should they alert the people on the island to their presence? How, then, would they steal the brass statue?

'Listen,' the second sea witch said, her voice barely above a whisper.

'I hear nothing,' the first answered impatiently. 'Not even the rustle of scorpions on sand.'

'Exactly. I suspect we've landed on a cursed island, one devoid of life. We must tread carefully,' the second sea witch said. 'Come, get the bottles. They look like they belong here.'

The two sea witches gathered the bottles in a bag. Passing by the man and his horse, they walked towards the city of brass.

The first sea witch was wrong. There was a single scorpion alive on the island. It scuttled towards the brass horse, and made an attempt to climb its leg. But, before it had the chance, the horse picked up that very same leg, and brought it down upon the scorpion.

And, very slowly, the scorpion too turned to brass.

❖

'How odd,' the first sea witch said to the second as they passed statues of people going about their day. At the door of one house a smiling mother waved goodbye to her children. The children waved back, their legs poised for a walk they would never begin.

Further in, guards patrolled the streets, laughing together; stallholders waved their wares and locals traded coins for goods.

The first sea witch approached one such stall, and peered closely at a set of coins that hung – as if by string, in mid-air – between the hands of a vendor and buyer. She reached out to touch one of the coins.

'Stop!' the second sea witch said.

But it was too late.

The hands slammed down, clasping one another, crushing the finger of the first sea witch. She screamed, and snatched it back, but it was too late. The very tip was coated in brass. The brass began to spread, until soon her whole finger was covered, followed by her hand.

'I'll turn to brass like the rest of them!' the first sea witch cried.

'No,' the second sea witch said. 'I won't let that happen. Follow me.'

They ran down the streets, boots slamming against brass. The brass crept up the first sea witch's wrist, like slithering snakes. It worked its way to her elbow, finally snaring her shoulder.

'I can hardly breathe,' she choked out, as the brass bloomed across her chest and neck. It moved to her stomach and legs, leaving her face until last. She would be forced to stand and watch as her body turned to brass before her eyes. 'And I can barely move.'

They had stopped just outside the gates of the palace. Surrounding the palace lay a moat, and surrounding the moat were brass-coated ivy plants.

'Wait here,' the second sea witch said, her voice shaking. 'I'll go inside and look for help.'

'Hurry,' were the last words spoken by the first sea witch, as brass coated her lips and silenced her.

The second sea witch rushed through the palace gates,

the bag of bottles jingling like bells. Inside everything was quiet.

She ran through the courtyard and into the throne room.

A brass king sat regally on a throne, cradling his brass baby, in front of a frozen crowd of guards and townspeople. The king was smiling down at the child, while the baby's mouth was parted mid-howl.

The second sea witch darted between the adoring crowds, hoping for a sign. Anything.

'Hello?' she called. The echo of her own voice taunted her.

Then she saw it.

Beside the throne stood a round table. The table resembled a clock face, with eight round holes where numerals should have stood. The sea witch dropped her bag to the ground and inspected the table closely.

At the very centre was, unmistakably, a drawing of a roc.

One of the bottles rolled out of the sea witch's bag. And, as she picked it up, she saw it was just the right size for the gap.

Could it be? the sea witch wondered.

She was used to magic and the clever ways it hid itself from the world. She was used to looking for it in strange places, unlocking it in unusual ways.

She placed the bottle in the gap in the table. Then she did the same with two more.

Suddenly a silver light shot from inside the bottles right up to the brass-coated ceiling. The second sea witch fell to the floor with the force of it, and covered her face with her arms.

When she looked back, three animals floated in the air above the three bottles. A cat with stripes like a tiger; a fish with scales that glinted gold; and a lizard, as dark as the night. The lizard and fish darted out of the room, trailing silver smoke. Only the cat was left behind.

It ignored the second sea witch, crawling instead over the shoulders of the king. It reached down to the brass baby and parted its mouth, sharp teeth bared.

The sea witch, overcome with a need to protect the child, cried out. She ran, preparing to pull the cat away. But the cat wasn't biting the baby's face. It was licking it. And each time its rough tongue met the baby's skin, some of the brass disappeared.

Some minutes passed before the baby's frozen cries filled the room. They echoed, furious, and the sea witch covered her ears. But the baby reached out a small hand for her, and its brown eyes glistened and shone like the stars.

When she gathered the baby in her arms, it stopped crying. She took one final look at its frozen father and knew she couldn't leave it there to perish.

The second sea witch left the throne room, with a gift greater than eight bottles made of brass. The cat followed closely behind. The rest of the bottles lay forgotten in her bag.

Outside the sea witch found her wife, her flesh restored.

'How did you free me? And why is there . . . a baby?'

'I'll explain soon,' the second sea witch said, caressing her wife's face. 'Let's leave this cursed island first.'

The two sea witches hurried away from the city, with a baby and a tiger-striped cat in exchange for eight brass bottles.

As they sailed away, the first sea witch asked, 'How long has it been since our lands saw a king?'

The second sea witch laughed, despite everything that had happened. 'A man ruling? It's been over a thousand years.'

They looked down at the child, whose glittering brown eyes were following the cat's twitching tail.

'The cat,' the second sea witch said. 'Do you think it could be . . .'

'A *jinni*?' the first answered.

The second sea witch nodded. 'I thought they were just a legend.'

'A strange magic has followed us home,' the first sea witch said, her voice heavy. 'And we must do everything we can to protect it.'

Chapter 16

When Jamila had finished telling the story, the room fell silent. Even Ramady, in the main cabin, knew not to make a sound.

'Was I the baby?' asked Amira.

'Yes,' said Jamila. 'You were our treasure. You and Namur.'

Instinctively, Amira tried to read her mother's emotions – but she saw nothing, smelled nothing. She had no power without her *jinni*. It was as if the magic that flowed through her veins whenever Namur was around had ceased to exist. Amira felt like a ghoul inhabiting someone else's life. All of the changes, all of these new truths, were too much to bear.

'If the king was my father –' Dunya flinched at Amira's words – 'and he ruled over one thousand years ago, does that mean I'm one thousand years old, too?'

'One thousand and twelve, I suppose,' said Jamila, her mouth twitching upwards in a half-smile.

Dunya looked at Amira anxiously, as if worried she might reject them.

Amira hadn't come from an oyster shell, and she wasn't born of the sea. That was just another one of her mother's stories. A fairy tale.

The truth was, Amira had a father.

Amira was angry with her mothers for keeping secrets from her. But right now, she had to focus on finding Namur. And so she swallowed her anger down, and laid out the pieces of the puzzle Leo and her mothers had given her.

The *jinn* had come from the brass city, and the roc was a type of *jinn*. But why had it been at the centre of the table? Was it somehow more important that the rest? And what had happened one thousand years ago to curse the people that lived there?

Amira had so many questions. She plucked out the biggest ones to ask her mothers, knowing that they would finally tell her the truth.

'Why did Namur only free *me* in the brass city?' Amira's heart jolted when she thought of her missing *jinni*. 'Why not the others?'

Dunya spoke this time. 'Namur chose you as his companion.'

'But then, how was Mama freed from the curse?' asked Amira.

Jamila studied her fingers, as if remembering that they had once been made of brass. 'We think it happened when Dunya released the magic by placing the bottles in the table.'

'And because the curse wasn't yet complete,' added Dunya.

'We have to go back and find a way to lift the curse!' Amira said passionately, thinking of her father, and the rest of the people on the island.

Dunya shook her head. 'We tried to return to the city of brass, but it had disappeared.'

'What do you mean? How can an island disappear?'

'We never found out,' said Dunya. 'And eventually, we stopped looking.'

'Is that why you never told me?' Amira asked, softening now. 'About my father?'

'Yes.' Jamila's voice was laced with emotion. 'We didn't want you to feel incomplete. Like you had to spend your life searching . . .'

'But we're sorry,' said Dunya. 'It was wrong of us.'

Amira tried to imagine her father now, and the city of brass where she had been born. Instead, she pictured Dunya's and Jamila's faces, and their dhow.

'It doesn't matter that I was born somewhere else,' she said at last. 'You, the dhow and Namur are home. And I'm going to find him.'

Her mothers' relief was like watching a flower bloom.

'What about the other *jinn*?' Amira asked. 'Where did they go?'

'I remember seeing the goldfish,' said Dunya. 'Which is why when Leo . . . well. You can imagine what a shock it was to see his *jinni*.'

'And the lizard?'

'It must have found a child of its own,' said Dunya.

'But there were eight *jinn*?' Amira pressed. 'And five remain in their bottles, still on the island?'

Jamila nodded.

Eight humans, five of them without their *jinn*. Amira couldn't imagine a world where she hadn't been paired with Namur.

'I think the stormbird on the horizon is the roc on that table,' she declared.

Dunya stared out of the window to where the stormbird slept. 'I think you're right,' she said.

Amira still didn't know why the stormbird was there, or how to stop it. She only knew that it would destroy their world if she didn't find the answers.

'There will be an answer,' said Jamila, as if reading her mind. 'We just need to know where to look.'

'I've been thinking,' began Dunya, uncertainly. 'There has been word of a midnight souk in the middle of the ocean. It is said to wash up all that has been lost at sea.'

'It's just a legend,' said Jamila dismissively. 'It would be a fool's errand to search for it.'

Amira frowned at her mother. 'You've been to a city of brass and you're not sure if a souk in the middle of the ocean is real? This is Namur we're talking about. We have to do everything we can to save him!'

Her mothers fell silent.

'You're right,' Jamila eventually said. 'Perhaps we've lost some of the spark we once had for sailing into the unknown.'

'And how I miss it,' added Dunya with a slight smile.

A spark of hope, like a stray ember, lit up inside Amira. 'Where is it?' She wanted to start charting their route right away.

Dunya frowned. 'Beneath the blood moon's beam. That's all the legend says.'

'But that's only three days away!' cried Amira, looking between her mothers. 'If we miss the blood moon, we'll miss the souk.'

'Well, then,' said Jamila. 'We had better start preparing.'

'I'll help!' Amira declared, standing up from her bed. But she suddenly felt dizzy and nauseated.

Jamila gently ushered her back. 'Rest,' she said. 'You can help later. All great adventures begin with a nap. You need to build up your strength.'

Amira was tired. So very tired. And her brain and heart hurt. They had a plan. For now that was enough.

She fell asleep to the feeling of Dunya's hands stroking her hair, and the sound of chickens clucking from the deck.

And the pain of losing Namur dulled, if only for a moment.

Chapter 17

Amira slept, on and off, all day, while Dunya ran the souk and Jamila prepared the dhow. But tonight it was her turn.

As the cabin turned dark, she pulled out the map she planned to use for their voyage. Amira had drawn the islands they had visited so far, though there weren't many.

Places with names she didn't know, scattered across the ocean like pebbles on a beach.

And somewhere, uncharted, was an island that held the midnight souk.

Amira studied the map, recounting where they had travelled, and imagining where they might still go. Her heart jolted when she saw a muddy paw print on Failaka. She had been angry at Namur, at the time, for dirtying her most prized possession. But she would tear the map to pieces if it meant having Namur by her side again.

Ramady left her corner and joined Amira on the cushion by the table, resting her head on her lap. It was as if she knew Amira's pain, sensed her loss. And though it wasn't the same, it gave her comfort.

With just a single candle to see what she was doing, Amira pulled a box the size of a book towards her, positioning it just in front of the map. The box was made of wood, painted with the sun and the moon. Only when she opened the box, did Amira blow the candle out.

Illuminated above her, hovering over the map, was the night sky, just as it appeared tonight. Most sailors used the sun and stars to navigate, but only sea witches could project them inside their cabins. And, instead of the stars and sun, Amira planned to use the moon. Tonight it was waxing, almost full, reminding her of the short time they had left.

On the inside lid of the box was a clockface, though it held more than just numbers. It held the position of the sun and the moon in the sky, and had three hands instead of two. Amira carefully turned the biggest one, painted silver, and watched as the sky above her in the cabin changed.

The moon sank, and the sun rose three times, until the blood moon hovered over her. Amira carefully turned the next two hands until they were positioned at the number twelve. Midnight. Only then did she turn back to her map, the moon and stars her only light source.

'Is that right?' Amira asked her mothers, after she called them in to show her findings.

Dunya frowned. 'It must be, though we've never come across an island there before.'

'Are you sure you set it right?' asked Jamila.

'Yes,' said Amira. 'Positive.'

Carefully, Amira positioned her pencil right where the

moon's beam fell. And she drew a star on the map to mark their destination, somewhere in the middle of the Gulf of Sahar.

◇✷◇

The next morning Amira woke, feeling nervous for the days ahead. As she carried out her chores in a daze, she imagined her life before her *jinni* had gone missing.

She had been hiding beneath the rowing boat, and his little head had peered under and nudged her foot. Amira had laughed, and Namur had started to turn invisible.

But she had trained herself to get angry *just enough* for him to appear again. It wasn't difficult.

Amira was often angry about lots of things: seagulls pooping on the dhow so she had to scrub the deck again, or the way the chickens clucked just before she wanted to wake. Once her mothers had to stop her chasing them with an axe. Then Amira was even angier because her mothers had teased her for getting angry at silly things like seagulls and chickens. Amira wasn't going to let herself get angry again. Ever.

Amira's anger had got her into plenty of trouble over the years. It was the reason she had rowed out to the stormbird after her argument with Leo. It was the reason Namur hadn't been able to turn invisible just as the stormbird snatched him up.

No. From now on she was going to be sweet, like the heroines she read about in stories.

When Amira was done with her chores, she sat with Ramady. The goat lay, unmoving, in her corner in the main cabin. Her belly was swollen and she was breathing heavily. Amira found the three cards Dunya had pulled from her deck tucked beneath one of Ramady's cushions.

She had forgotten them, and she thought about them now.

The Lovers. The Fool. Death.

The cards had known what would happen. They had foreseen that her life would change forever because she would lose someone close. And they had known it would happen at Amira's own foolishness.

Amira hoped this wasn't the end of her story. She hoped there was more to come. She hoped she could alter her fate.

Her eyes were drawn to the two intertwined mermaids. And she remembered, for the first time since she had been dragged under the water that terrible night, about the mermaids who had rescued her. Had they been the sisters from the island of rocs? How had they found her?

She tucked the cards beneath the pillow in her cabin, hoping they would grant her safe passage.

Amira and Jamila stood at the deck of the dhow, looking out at the port, as was their custom. Except they usually weren't as solemn as they were today.

As Dunya began to steer them away, Amira felt the dhow beneath her begin to move. She took a deep breath – as was *her* custom – to remember the smells of Failaka. Smoke, fresh fish and something beneath it all.

Something she could no longer read.

Amira wondered when they would next see the island, if they would ever come back. And she wondered, briefly, about Leo. Should she have visited him to say goodbye?

Amira watched the crowd on the dock, rushing from one place to the next like worker ants. There were fewer of them today, as people chose to stay indoors. Still, they knew where they belonged. Amira didn't. Her life, as she knew it, had been ripped from under her. It felt as if she was at the whim of the ocean waves. Her father kept sneaking into her mind. Did they share the same eyes or taste for goat's milk? Did they both hate mornings and love the sunset?

Amira was distracted by a flash of sandy hair on the dock, moving a beat quicker, out of time with the rest of the crowd. It was as if her thoughts of Leo had summoned him there.

'Amira!' Leo yelled. 'Amira, wait!'

'Mama, stop!' Amira called up to Dunya.

Dunya glanced down. 'What is it?'

'Stop!' Amira called again.

Leo was sprinting along the dock, Semek in his arms. And he looked just about ready to launch himself from the wharf right on to the dhow.

Chapter 18

'What's he doing here?' Dunya asked from the steering wheel. 'I can't bring the dhow any closer, not with the waves as they are.'

Amira stared down at Leo. He seemed desperate to see her. She couldn't leave the dhow, not when they had such an important journey ahead of them. But maybe he had information that could help her find Namur. She hesitated, caught between Leo and her mothers, land and sea. Torn between two worlds.

'Wait!' She turned to her mothers with an idea. 'Let him on. I'm going to fetch a rope and a basket.'

Leo seemed to have heard her. He grinned from the port wall. Dunya held the wheel firm.

Ramady wandered out of the cabin and peered at Leo through the rails. Amira grabbed a rope, tied it round the mast, and pulled it along to the edge of the dhow. Then she slipped a basket on the rope. She looked up at Leo, who hadn't taken his eyes off her.

'Catch!' she said, holding the end of the rope ready.

Leo put Semek's bowl down and held his arms out, eyes wide.

'Don't worry,' said Amira, and she threw the rope to him.

Leo caught it, stumbling backwards. 'What do I do now?' he called.

'I'm going to slide the basket down to you,' Amira explained. 'Put Semek and your bag in it first and slide them back to me. Then it's your turn.'

Leo looked down at the water as if it were a pit of fire waiting to burn him. But then he looked back up at Amira and nodded.

Amira slid the basket down the rope. Leo put Semek's bowl inside, as Amira had instructed. The *jinni* darted left and right, spinning around his bowl like a compass point. Then Leo placed his bag next to the bowl.

'Now throw the end of the rope back to me,' said Amira. 'And hold tight to the bit on your end.'

Leo did as he was told. Amira pulled the rope, Semek sliding along, until he was safely on board.

'How am *I* supposed to get on?' asked Leo as Amira handed the bag and Semek to Jamila.

Amira pursed her lips. 'Can you swim?'

Five minutes later Amira and Jamila dragged a soaking-wet Leo on board.

'Hi, Leo,' said Amira..

'Hello,' replied Leo, suddenly shy.

'Did you have something to tell me?'

Leo took a breath. 'Just . . .'

'Well?' Amira persisted. 'Go on!'

She remembered she was trying to be sweet these days, like the characters she read about in books, and she bit her tongue. It was *really* hard not to get angry sometimes.

Dunya coughed. 'Sorry to interrupt, but we have to go now if we're to make it to the midnight souk.'

Amira tapped her foot on the deck, looking at Leo. 'Well?' she said again, as sweetly as she could.

'Where's Namur?' said Leo, looking around.

Any hope of sweetness seeped out of Amira. 'He's gone,' she said shortly.

And she told him about rowing out to sea to search for answers, and the stormbird, and about how it had plucked

Namur like a berry from a bush. Her heart ached as she explained it all again. 'We're going to find answers,' she said. 'So, tell me what you came to say, and then you have to go.'

Leo tilted his head and looked at her. 'No.'

Amira was still trying not to get angry. She pinched the bridge of her nose with her forefinger and thumb, the way Jamila did whenever she was annoyed, and she said, 'Leo, we need to leave.'

'I know,' said Leo. 'I'm coming with you. I'm going to help you find Namur.'

In the distance thunder roared. The stormbird flapped its wings, hovering above its nest, before sinking down again. It seemed restless. Hungry.

Leo pulled out a notebook from his pocket and wrote something down.

'What are you doing?' asked Amira curiously.

'Keeping track of its movements. Trying to see a pattern,' explained Leo. 'That's what scientists do.'

'We need to set sail now,' said Jamila, placing an arm on both of their shoulders. Dunya had taken her place by the wheel again.

Amira turned to her mother. 'Leo's coming with us,' she said, a smile tweaking the corners of her mouth. 'He's going to help us find Namur.'

Jamila scrutinized Leo, as if deciding whether he would cope with the voyage. Then she nodded. 'Good. He can be our lookout,' she said, 'now that you're navigating.' And she waltzed back into the cabin without another word.

While Dunya sailed them away from Failaka port, and Jamila returned to her favourite task – mixing tonics – Amira gave Leo a tour of the cabin. She warned him to stay away from Ramady's corner, and showed him some of her favourite books and the tapestries she knotted to sell at the souk.

When they were done, Amira and Leo positioned themselves at the table, each on their own cushion. Semek sat in the middle between them.

Leo reached into his bag. Amira could see the metal sphere he had showed her, and other things she didn't recognize. As she watched, he pulled out a parcel wrapped in brown paper and a neatly tied ribbon. Leo blushed as he handed it to Amira.

'I . . . I got you a present,' he said.

Amira stared at the present. Slowly, carefully, she began to unwrap it. As soon as she saw the flash of red, she realized it was the music box from Leo's house.

'I'm sorry,' Leo said as she inspected it. 'I shouldn't have got angry at you. I was just . . .'

It was the first time Amira had been given a gift by a friend, and she wanted to offer him something in return.

'I know,' she said, giving him her understanding. 'I get angry too.'

Leo smiled gratefully. 'You can carry it around with you,' he explained, turning his attention to the radio. 'And listen to music wherever you go.'

He stopped talking, his ears turning pink as he peered at Amira.

'Thank you,' Amira said. 'I love it.'

And, surprising herself, she pulled Leo in for a hug.

Chapter 19

It didn't take long for the group to settle into their roles. Amira took over the table in the cabin, laying out the map and equipment she would use to chart their route.

'What's this?' asked Leo, studying the box Amira had used the night before.

'It helps us chart our course, using the moon, sun and stars,' explained Amira. Then she showed him her map and pointed out the location of the midnight souk.

From a velvet cloth the colour of sea foam, Amira pulled out a small replica of *Tigerheart* and placed it on the map to match their position. As she showed Leo the route they would take, the map came to life.

The faded blue of the ocean turned brighter. It ebbed and flowed, like waves, and the miniature *Tigerheart* began to sail along. Just above the little dhow hung a mist, like clouds, which hovered over the table. The star shot up to the sky, and formed a constellation that looked like a cat's nose and whiskers.

Leo's jaw dropped. He crouched down to look at the tiny dhow up close.

'It's moving!' he said. 'And the sea . . . it's alive!'

Amira grinned. 'It helps us keep track of our position.'

As they watched the dhow sail together, Leo and Amira discussed the stormbird.

'Why did it take Namur?' he asked.

Amira shook her head. 'Maybe because I was trying to reach its nest?'

'And did you?' Leo asked, his eyes wide.

'No,' said Amira, before continuing. 'I couldn't get closer to it, no matter how far I sailed. It kept moving away, like the horizon.'

'So, we can't reach the stormbird,' Leo concluded. 'But it can reach us?'

Amira nodded.

'Then why didn't it take *you*?'

Amira sighed. 'It went for Namur first. But before I could do anything something pulled me into the water.' Then she told Leo about the mermaids, and how they had dragged her to shore.

'Do you think it's after *jinn*?' Leo asked, peering at Semek who was perched on his lap.

'I don't know,' Amira admitted. 'But I do know we have to be careful. If we're out at sea, it might attack again.'

'It won't work!' Jamila interrupted, emerging in an acrid-smelling cloud of smoke from her cabin. 'The flower burns before I get the chance to extract its essence.'

Leo peered through the open door at Jamila's vials and beakers, all of various sizes, each connected to a glass tube. Beside them all was a smoking pot.

'Have you tried covering it in a substance to protect it?' Leo suggested.

Jamila narrowed her eyes suspiciously. 'How do you know about this craft?'

'Sorry,' Leo muttered, turning pink. 'I'm interested in science and sometimes I like to mix –'

Jamila marched back into her cabin and slammed the door shut.

Amira smiled at Leo. 'Don't worry,' she said. 'It's not you. She's like this when she's in the middle of a new mix.'

Leo nodded. 'Now I know where you get it from.'

Amira smiled at him in surprise. 'It's true,' she said with a shrug, turning her attention back to the map.

Some time later Jamila emerged again. 'It worked this time,' she said, holding a pale pink tonic in her hands as if it were the cure to all disease and famine. 'You,' she pointed at Leo. 'Come here.'

Amira nodded at Leo, encouraging him. He obediently joined Jamila in the next cabin.

Then Amira slipped out of the cabin and on to the

deck to update Dunya on their position.

If they were lucky, and if legend was true, they would reach the midnight souk just as the sun set on their second day of sailing.

So long as the weather stayed fair and the stormbird didn't attack.

Chapter 20

'How are you feeling?' Jamila asked Leo as the group sat down for their evening meal.

Leo looked even paler than usual, which was saying a lot. Semek, who hadn't turned invisible at all since Leo stepped on the dhow, watched him with unblinking eyes. 'Not great,' he admitted.

At some point in the afternoon the seas had turned rough. The dhow rocked violently from side to side, and the waves reached all the way to the windows.

Amira and her mothers were used to it, moving with the motion of the dhow, but Leo wasn't. He had spent most of the afternoon lying on Amira's bed, head stuffed beneath the pillow.

'Drink this,' said Jamila. 'It'll help. I promise,' she added, when Leo looked at the green concoction with barely disguised disgust.

'It doesn't taste as bad as it looks,' Amira said, hoping

he wouldn't read her lie.

The further they travelled, the more the stormbird's current crackled through the air, which hummed as if the dhow was sailing in the middle of a beehive.

Leo drank the concoction Jamila gave him in one big gulp.

'Oh . . .!' said Amira. 'You're supposed to sip it.'

Leo covered his mouth with a gloved hand.

'Why do you think Leo wears those gloves?' Amira had whispered to Dunya earlier that day.

'Why don't you ask him?'

'He yelled at me last time.'

'Why don't you ask him *nicely*?' Dunya had said.

Amira had glowered. 'I'm always nice!' Wasn't she?

Leo rushed out of the cabin now, still holding his hands to his mouth. He returned five minutes later, looking worse than ever. He pointed at Amira accusingly.

'You said it doesn't taste bad!'

Amira tried not to laugh. 'I'm sorry. I was trying to help.'

'Shall we try some goat's milk to wash it down?' Jamila offered.

While Leo sipped his goat's milk, Jamila served stuffed

cabbage leaves in a tomato sauce: Amira's favourite. The meal, sitting there together, reminded her miserably of Namur. If he were here, she thought, he would nibble at the meat and sample the leftover sauce when no one was looking. And even though he wasn't there, she saved some food for him, as she always had.

◇✦◇

After dinner, Amira and Leo discussed their theories about the stormbird, and where it might have taken Namur.

'You said that without a human, *jinn* are always invisible,' began Amira. 'So why hasn't Namur escaped and found me?'

'I don't know,' Leo said in frustration. They had returned to the subject over and over, and didn't seem any closer to a solution. 'And I don't understand why the stormbird isn't attacking us now when it attacked you before.'

They gazed out of the cabin window at the stormbird's nest.

'Let's count our lucky stars,' said Amira. She gazed at Semek swirling round and round his bowl. 'Leo?'

'Yes?'

'Are you nervous?'

Leo frowned. 'Well, I was earlier. Getting on the dhow, and setting sail. I've never been on the ocean before –'

Amira interrupted him. 'Yes, but are you nervous *now*?'

'Not really. Why?'

'Then why is Semek visible? Has he disappeared at all since the storm arrived and the stormbird appeared on the horizon?'

Leo looked uncertain. 'Now that you mention it, no.'

Amira nodded, buzzing with excitement. 'Namur stopped turning invisible after the storm too. I thought it was because I was angry. I thought the night he disappeared was because of me, because I couldn't make him turn invisible and save himself. But . . .'

'It's the current!' Leo declared. 'Of course! The current from the stormbird is confusing them.' He pulled out his notebook. 'We're getting there!'

Amira still didn't know where Namur was, or why the stormbird had taken him. But at least she knew now that it wasn't her anger that had made him vulnerable, and that relief was enough to keep her going.

'Who's going to tell a story tonight?' asked Dunya.

Amira usually begged for a turn. She loved telling stories. But it didn't feel the same without Namur, as most of her stories involved him.

'What do you mean?' asked Leo. The waves had eased a little, and the colour had returned to his face.

Jamila explained their custom of exchanging stories in the evenings.

'Real ones, or made-up ones?' asked Leo.

'It can be either. Or a mixture.'

'Would you like to have a turn this evening?' Dunya asked Leo.

'Yes!' Amira cried, wriggling in her seat. 'Please share a story.'

'Oh,' said Leo nervously, clearing his throat. 'Sure. I suppose.'

'Wonderful,' said Jamila. 'Amira, would you like to bring out the bakhoor and show Leo how to light it?'

Amira hopped up. 'You can pick your own scent,' she explained, pulling a box out. Leo selected the orange, as she had known he would, and placed a single perfumed wood chip on top of a lit piece of coal.

'Now what?' he asked.

'Now you dance!'

Ramady slid closer to the table. She always joined in on the stories, though Amira was never certain she understood them.

When the smoke had settled above them, Leo cleared his throat.

'This story is real,' he said, eyes darting around the cabin. Eventually, they rested on Amira. 'It all began on a sunny afternoon, when a sailor, a schoolteacher and their son were huddled together . . .'

The Tale of the Sailor and his Family

'I'll be back soon,' the sailor said to his son. His voice was sickly sweet, like sugar pastries.

They were standing at the busy port, fishermen loading their dhows for a day at sea.

The little boy, who was no older than three or four, reached for his father, eyes filled with tears. His mother, the schoolteacher, crouched by his side to comfort him.

'Where are you going?' the little boy asked his father.

'Out to sea,' the sailor said.

'But I want you to stay,' said the boy.

The sailor crouched down and looked into his son's eyes. The pair of them were identical. Only time separated their features, hardening the sailor's skin and hair.

'I must go,' the sailor insisted, a little impatiently now. 'How else will I look after you and your mother?'

The schoolteacher's lips tightened. 'I work too,' she

said, but, seeing her son was watching her, she smiled. 'Safe journey,' she said, her voice clipped and cold.

'Remember, my boy,' the sailor said. 'If you're ever lost at sea, all you need to do is sing our song.'

The boy was too young to understand his father's advice, and so he simply nodded, happy to have two parents who loved him so much.

The sailor hugged the schoolteacher. She stood stiffly until he pulled away. Afterwards she reached for her son's hand, softening like butter left in the sun. She pulled him into her arms, nuzzling her cheek to his, as they watched the sailor board his dhow.

'We make a good team, don't we?' the schoolteacher said to her son as the sailor left the port.

The little boy nodded. 'You, me and Baba.'

In the distance the sky turned grey and the sun began to dip into the horizon. The sailor's dhow, now the size of an apple, had almost disappeared, as he chased whatever lay beyond.

'Come on,' the schoolteacher said. 'Let's go home and have some dinner. We can read your very *favourite* story tonight.'

But the boy had walked to the edge of the port, where all the dhows were stationed, neat as ducks. He bent down and dunked his hand into the waves.

'Be careful!' The schoolteacher pulled the boy's hand from the water. 'You'll crush your fingers if the waves bring the dhows too close.'

'Mama, look!' the little boy said. 'Gold!'

The schoolteacher peered into the water. 'Where?' she asked curiously. 'What do you see?'

The schoolteacher had once loved adventure and uncertainty. When they were younger, she and the sailor had voyaged together across oceans, discovering new places, seeing strange creatures and witnessing magic. She knew how to tie knots, how to steer a dhow and how to read the stars. The sea had been, for so many years, an extension of her legs.

Then she fell pregnant. She and the sailor agreed to stay on the next island they discovered and build a life together on land. That's when they had stumbled upon Failaka.

She found a job she loved, as a schoolteacher, and raised their son happily. And every evening, after her husband had gone to bed, she mapped out the first voyage they would take together as a family.

But her husband was restless, and he would not wait for his son to grow.

'I have heard tale of ever-moving islands filled with riches for those willing to find them. I can search for them while you look after our boy, and return in time for the winter.'

The idea infected the sailor like an illness. It spread first from his dreams to his mind. When it reached his heart, the schoolteacher knew he was lost to her.

'There, Mama!' the little boy said, bursting through the schoolteacher's thoughts like a dog over a puddle.

In the water swam a fish made of gold. It swam to the surface, touching the tip of its nose to the boy's finger.

'Can we keep it, Mama?' he asked.

The fish darted down into the

water when the schoolteacher bent in for a closer look, peeking out only for her son. Perhaps it was a good omen. Something to protect the boy from the hardships that would follow.

'Of course,' the schoolteacher said. 'What shall we call it?'

The boy thought carefully.

'Semek,' he said. 'We'll call him Semek.'

Chapter 21

'When I realized Baba wasn't going to come back, I started wearing the gloves,' Leo explained. 'I saw Mama get ill, very ill, after he left. It was my way of not catching the illness. I didn't understand at the time that it wasn't the sort of illness you could catch. When I got older and learned to read emotions, it started to make sense.

But it got worse. Suddenly, there were things I couldn't touch at all without my gloves. Doorknobs, food, other people.'

Leo fidgeted with his gloved hands.

'I try not to wear them. But I like to carry them around, in case I need them. Usually I only wear them when I'm extra nervous.'

He pulled them off and stuffed them in his pocket, glancing up at Amira with a look of shame.

'When you met me,' said Amira, 'I was carrying sea water around in a pouch. It was like a lucky charm. Maybe your gloves are like that? Maybe they're a kind of magic?'

'Maybe,' Leo said, though his voice was sad.

'Your mother,' said Dunya softly. 'Does she know you're here?'

Leo sighed. 'I didn't want to tell you that night, Amira . . . It's why I got so angry. She's not at home now. She's somewhere she can heal. She won't be back for a while.'

Amira thought Leo seemed uncertain of whether she would be back at all.

'I'm glad you're with us, Leo,' said Jamila. 'Your mother will be so proud when she hears you've been on your first voyage.'

Leo's face lit up. 'She will be! It's just . . .'

'I know,' said Dunya. 'Some wounds, though we can't see them, take longer to heal. It's good that your mother is facing how she feels. Not everyone is brave enough to do that.'

Amira couldn't imagine what Leo had gone through. She felt so lucky to have two mothers by her side . . . And a father too, though she would never have the chance to meet him.

Perhaps fathers weren't something she and Leo would

ever know. But that was OK. Families come in all shapes and sizes. All that matters is that they love you, and you love them back. Amira loved her mothers, and Namur, and Ramady, and the chickens. And she could imagine loving Leo too. He slotted into their life like he had always been there. Namur was her companion, but Leo was quickly becoming her best friend.

'Well, I have a spare mother, if you want one,' Amira eventually said, and Leo laughed.

'Hey!' said Jamila. 'Don't be giving us up too quickly.'

'Which one of us do you prefer?' said Dunya, teasing.

'Don't answer that,' said Jamila. 'You don't have to choose.'

Far away the stormbird perched at its nest, gathering its energy, and Amira rested, preparing herself for the voyage ahead.

Chapter 22

Their second day at sea was their roughest, and the animals were restless. The chickens paced the dhow, clucking, while Ramady's nest in the cabin had transformed into a fort.

'I wonder if she's going to have her young?' said Jamila, frowning at Ramady. 'Oh, but it's *such* bad timing!'

The barometer spun wildly, just as it had during the storm that took them to Failaka, and the night Namur went missing.

The stormbird lay awake in its nest. In the darkness you might almost miss it, but for its eyes like stars, watching, silent.

Rain had scattered on and off all day, wind whipping everyone's faces. It was only when the sun began to set that the clouds parted and gave way to the blood moon.

It shone big and bright, its light reflected in the ocean's surface. Amira leaned over the rails and looked out at it and, for a moment, it was as if she were floating through the sky. She closed her eyes and breathed in the sea air. Licking her lips, she tasted salt. And she convinced herself that, by the end of the night, she would be reunited with Namur again.

Leo was in the crow's nest, keeping a lookout. Amira climbed up to join him. Halfway up, she could hear singing. She wondered whether it was another music box, but then she realized the song was coming from Leo.

Amira paused, and she listened.

It was a sailor's song, one Amira had heard before. But she had only heard it from the mouths of gruff men, their voices coarse and hard. Leo's voice was like a songbird's, and Amira could almost see each note float towards her, delicate as a petal.

When he was done, Amira climbed into the crow's nest to join him and Semek.

'That was beautiful,' she said.

Leo jumped when he heard her voice. His ears turned pink at once. 'Oh!' he said, flustered. 'I just . . . It helps with the sea sickness.'

Amira grinned. 'You have a very good voice,' she said.

'That's not a compliment; it's just a fact.'

Leo laughed.

'Look! The moon came out for you,' said Amira, pointing into the distance.

Leo smiled. 'I can feel it, like a force, pulling me.'

'Me too,' said Amira. She fidgeted with something on her lap. 'I made you something,' she said, holding a piece of threaded rope out to Leo. She had tied knots into patterns, all gathering at the bottom, like a pouch. She had threaded a diamond pattern all the way around the bag, in blue rope that Jamila had helped her dye to match the sea.

'What is it?' Leo asked.

'I'll show you.' Amira picked up Semek's bowl and placed it inside the pouch. Then she slung the top of the rope over her shoulder. 'Now you don't have to carry Semek around in your arms. But he can still see out.'

'It's perfect!' said Leo, his eyes shining. 'Thank you.'

'That's OK,' said Amira, suddenly feeling a little shy.

She wanted to show Leo that she was grateful for him being there. She wanted to thank him for being her friend, and show him that he was a part of their family.

'The stormbird is watching us,' said Leo after a pause.

The roc was curled into itself in its nest, like a dying fire.

'Why doesn't it just attack us?' Amira thought aloud.

'I wonder if it's waiting for something?' said Leo.

'For what?' asked Amira.

'I suppose we'll see.' Leo didn't sound nervous any more. He sounded confident, and sure. 'I just want to know why it's here.'

A thought fluttered through Amira's mind, like a butterfly. Something the woman had said at the souk that day, about holding our feelings inside.

'You know how our *jinn* come to us when we're feeling things?' she said. 'Namur comes when I'm angry, Semek comes when you're nervous. What if each *jinni* represents each human emotion, and they all feed *into* the stormbird? So it's always around because everyone is always feeling emotions. Except they're hiding it.'

Amira told Leo about everything she had seen, smelled and felt on land. About the way everyone buried their feelings deep inside.

'Maybe the stormbird is here because everyone is hiding

how they feel. You said, in science, everything has to go somewhere. What if the stormbird is where all of the emotions are going?'

Leo's eyes widened. 'So, *everyone* is the stormbird's human?' he said. 'Everyone in the Sahar Peninsula?'

Amira nodded.

Leo pulled out his notebook, scribbling fast. 'It could explain why it's never invisible, and why the current is always around. Because all the people are keeping their emotions locked inside. Amira, I think we might have cracked it!'

Amira grinned. 'I did science!' she said proudly.

Leo laughed. 'Now we know why the stormbird is here, we just need to figure out how to stop it causing all of this trouble.'

'And find Namur,' added Amira. The thrill at solving the puzzle – or part of it – filled her with confidence. And she felt, for a brief moment, as if it might all work out.

'I was thinking,' said Leo after some time. He sounded nervous. 'If this souk helps you find things that are lost, well . . . do you think I might be able to find my dad?'

Amira bit her lip. 'I don't know,' she said. She held

back the truth that was swimming through her mind. Sailing was dangerous, especially for those who travelled alone. Many sailors never made it back. It was a reality she and her mothers had lived with their whole lives, but it was one Leo wasn't accustomed to.

Amira's thoughts shifted to her own father again, trapped in the city of brass, out there somewhere, hidden just out of sight. It was strange to know you had family you would never meet. She understood a little what Leo was going through.

She placed an arm round Leo and leaned her head on his shoulder. 'If he is out there,' she said. 'I hope we find him.'

They watched the reflection of the moonlight bouncing off the water. And then, rather suddenly, Leo stirred.

'Look!' he said, standing up. 'Over there!'

In the distance Amira saw a great dhow several times the size of her own. It was three storeys high, unlike anything she had seen before, and was painted purple and gold. The top deck was open to the sky.

'That's it!' she cried. 'The midnight souk isn't an island at all. It's a *dhow*!'

Chapter 23

Amira and Leo scrambled down on to the deck. But as they sailed closer, they saw the great dhow ahead of them was empty, as if abandoned.

'Is this really it?' Amira asked her mothers as they leaned over the railings to look.

Dunya frowned. 'Perhaps we missed it, and everyone's gone?'

Surrounding the great dhow were others, just like *Tigerheart*. They were all empty too.

Amira's heart thudded. 'We can't have missed it. We can't be too late . . . It's still the blood moon!'

'Don't worry,' said Jamila, placing a hand on Amira's arm. 'We'll –'

But before she could finish her sentence, they heard a voice call out from the ocean.

Amira thought at first that it was a mermaid. But as the group peered over the rails, they saw a woman in a rowing boat. She looked to be the same age as Amira's mothers, with darker skin, and hair as long as Jamila's.

'What is your purpose?' she asked.

'We came in search of the midnight souk,' said Jamila.

The woman nodded. 'I can take you there.'

Amira frowned. 'But the dhow seems empty,' she said.

'Not quite,' the woman said, offering no further explanation. 'In order to enter the midnight souk, you must first pay a fee.'

Jamila reached into her pouch to pull out some coins. The woman waved her away.

'A story,' she explained. 'One of you must tell a story. If it is good enough, you shall pass. If it is not, you must leave.'

Amira's heart thudded. They had come so far to find Namur. What would they do if they were turned away? How would they begin to search for him? But she brushed aside her worries like dust. She and her mothers fed on stories. They were as certain as the rising sun.

'OK,' said Amira. 'I'll do it.'

The woman faced Amira, eyebrows raised. 'Are you sure?'

'Yes,' said Amira, more decisively this time. It was her *jinni* they were here to find, after all, and she would trust no one but herself.

She told the story of her and Namur's first adventure together on the island of rocs, where they had met the mermaid sisters. Amira looked past the woman, and imagined she was telling the story to Namur.

She imagined they were in her room again, and he was sitting there, tail curled round his body, watching her. She could feel him on the back of her neck, his body warm, his whiskers tickling her cheeks. And she imagined all of the other adventures they would have together once he was back safe.

When Amira was finished with her story the woman narrowed her eyes. And she nodded.

She rowed them towards the midnight souk in silence. Amira watched the rowing boat slide over the ocean, as smooth as silk and as black as ink. The blood moon shone above them, casting a red haze over the dhow.

'It only appears in the moonlight,' the woman explained. 'By sunrise it will be gone.'

As soon as the boat sailed beneath the light of the

moon, the midnight souk came to life.

Hundreds of voices broke the silence, making Amira jump. Leo's mouth dropped open like a fish. Smoke billowed out of the dhow in colourful clouds, and Amira imagined them taking the shape of all the stories shared and told. From within the souk came smells of perfume and fresh food. Amira's mouth watered, and she felt a hum of excitement that had nothing to do with the current crackling from the stormbird.

Moments later they stepped aboard the midnight souk. Amira heard Leo suck in his breath.

'The smell is so powerful,' he said. He was carrying Semek in the bag Amira had made him, and the fish *jinni* was darting around his bowl. 'Everyone is so . . . alive.'

Amira didn't need her powers to sense the energy of the sailors around her. These people were nothing like the people on land. They laughed, they argued and they felt everything as much on the outside as they did on the inside.

Being around them felt like coming home.

Amira and Leo followed Jamila and Dunya down the

first row of stalls, where bodies swam as one, like a school of fish. Unlike the regular souk, each stall in this place held lost items waiting to be found. Giant oyster shells that only opened for those pure of heart. Paintings that seemed to move when no one was looking, pulled from the wreckage of a dhow. Locked cases, with missing keys, filled with objects unknown.

Instead of money and goods, the vendors asked for stories. People told tales of cities buried in the sand, ghouls that stole your face, and mirages designed to trick unsuspecting travellers.

'Why stories?' asked Leo. 'Why not coins?'

'Because stories are a form of magic,' said Dunya.

'And those who know how to harness them,' added Jamila, 'will be richer than coins could offer.'

They snaked around the first floor, voices surrounding them, smells enveloping them, until they were sure they had scoured every stall. A set of wooden stairs took them up to the next level.

Up here, it was a little different, the magic wilder.

'Be careful,' warned Dunya as they walked around. 'They have altered these objects. They might be dangerous, unchecked. Everything must have rules. Even magic.'

Pink foam bubbled from a boiling pot behind a table, where a woman was busy stirring and filling heart-shaped bottles. A sign at the front of the stall read: *One drop a day mixed with the lost hair of your intended and they will love you for eternity.*

Amira knew, from watching Jamila mix for so many years, that the woman must have crushed rose petals and mixed it with a special gas for the effect.

'You should never toy with the minds of others,' muttered Jamila, disapprovingly, as they passed. Amira couldn't help but think of the tonics her mother made and sold. Was toying with emotions any better?

Further in, there were stalls with clothes that promised the wearer beauty, and books filled with spells that required a sacrifice to be performed. Amira read some of the sacrifices, and they made her stomach churn.

The whisper of a snake.

The song of a whale.

The cry of a newborn.

'Come closer, girl,' said a woman from the stall opposite. Amira felt Leo stiffen, but he moved with her towards the stall nonetheless.

This stall was filled with cages. Amira peered inside to see what they held. Animals, cruelly snared. She felt a lump in her stomach, like she had swallowed a rock. Could Namur be in there, afraid and alone? She would know, wouldn't she? She would feel him . . .

Turtles with reflective shells stared up at them dolefully.

'If you looked closely at their glistening scales, you might just discover your biggest misfortune,' said the woman. 'And here we have toads with venom so powerful it could kill you within seconds. To become immune you must swallow one whole, and let it live inside your stomach for the rest of your life.'

But Namur was not there. Amira was both disappointed and relieved. She didn't trust the woman.

There were miniature birds that turned to dust whenever they were touched, said to grant you luck.

'Would you like one?' the woman offered. 'I'll trade for your *jinni.*' She smiled a hungry smile at Leo this time. Amira took a step back and pulled Leo – who was clutching Semek close to him – with her.

'What a shame . . .' The woman shrugged lazily, already

turning to the next trader.

Amira and Leo wound their way back through the souk several times before returning to the start. There was now a line in front of the stall that sold love potions, and a girl with what looked like a lizard in her hair almost collided with them as they tried to squeeze through

'Sorry,' she muttered, barely glancing at them before rushing past.

'Where have my mothers gone?' asked Amira, irritably, when they were safely away from the stall. She knew that if Namur was able to get to her, he would find her here, at the midnight souk. But so far she hadn't seen so much as a hint of him. And they only had one more level left to explore.

'There you are!' said Jamila, rushing up behind her. 'We were worried when we lost you!'

She hugged Amira tight as if she wanted to never let go. Amira pulled herself away, scowling. Angry tears slid down her face.

Dunya reached out for her. 'What's wrong?'

'Everything!' Amira said, garnering the attention of a few nosy passers-by. 'I thought we would find Namur here, but we've found *nothing*.'

Amira's mothers and Leo looked at her with concern. But right now, their sympathy was driving her mad. She didn't need them to tiptoe around her, or worry she might break.

'Amira,' said Jamila, pulling her into a quiet corner. 'You need to calm down; it won't help. I have this tonic here; why don't you –'

'No!' said Amira.

She thought about the people on Failaka, and how she had read their emotions, and how they wanted Jamila's vials to stop them from feeling. And yet, on the outside, they showed nothing. Was that what happened when you grew older? Did you hide parts of yourself from the world?

Amira realized it was what she had been doing with her own emotions. She fought against her anger, even though it lived inside her. She could feel it spark, like a fire, and she tried hard not to let it out. But sometimes it felt that if she held it in, the fire would light within her. It felt as if the spark would spread through her insides and she would turn to ash.

Amira was beginning to doubt whether Jamila's tonics

were always helpful. Wasn't Leo's nervousness the reason he could read emotions through Semek? And wasn't he caring and kind and thoughtful, too? How would all of that change if he wasn't nervous any more?

Amira was angry, yes, but she was passionate. And determined. Would those things go away if she didn't feel mad sometimes? And if she held her anger in, would she only make the stormbird stronger? If it really was feeding off everyone's emotions – growing stronger each time they hid their true feelings – then her mothers were guilty of helping it.

'Our tonics stop people feeling things,' Amira finally said. 'That's what we do. We trade feelings for food and clothes. We make them drink cordials and tonics to stop them worrying. Or –' she continued, her words tumbling over one another – 'we smell how they're feeling and frighten them with what we know. This . . . all of it, has to stop.'

'Ami–' Dunya began, but Amira pressed on.

'I *need* to feel sad. I *need* to feel angry. Because it's those feelings that are going to help me save Namur.' The strength in her voice shattered as she spoke his name. 'It's those feelings that will help me fix this. If I stop feeling, how will I remember what it's like when he perches on my shoulder, or tickles my cheek with his whiskers, or digs his paws into me when he's afraid? If I stop feeling, how will I remember how much I love him? That I would go to the ends of the earth for him?'

Amira's mothers were silent.

Suddenly something crashed into the side of the giant dhow, rocking it back and forth like a swing.

Everyone at the midnight souk screamed. And Amira saw it, like a cannon.

The stormbird.

Chapter 24

The dhow turned to chaos.

People ran towards the exit, scrambling to get on to rowing boats. The stormbird pulled back after the first attack and turned towards each of the dhows parked around the midnight souk. It picked up some of the smaller ones in its claws and flew to a great height, before dropping them into the ocean like pebbles.

Amira, her mothers and Leo joined the panicked crowd. From the stairs came smoke, creeping towards them, creating a haze over everything.

Fire.

Amira whipped her head round to search for the source, just as her mothers launched themselves into a rowing boat. A few people jumped into the water to escape the flames, and were immediately swallowed up by the waves.

'Come on, Amira,' shouted Dunya as Leo stepped into the rowing boat too. 'Hurry!' She looked more afraid than she had the night the storm had driven them to Failaka.

Amira was about to step into the boat when she saw the girl with the lizard in her hair again. She was moving *up* the dhow, in the opposite direction to everyone else, towards the fire.

Something nagged at Amira. A piece of information she was missing.

The lizard nuzzled into the girl's hair while she rushed on, the way Namur wrapped himself round Amira's shoulders, and that's when Amira realized. It was a *jinni*. The third *jinni* released on the island of brass was here, at the midnight souk!

'Get in the boat, Amira!' Jamila begged.

Amira tore her eyes away from the girl, towards Leo and her mothers. People were pushing and shoving at her, desperate to get off, away from the fire. Leo looked at Amira with wide eyes. He could see the battle raging inside her.

'Hurry, Amira!' cried Dunya.

What if the lizard girl knew how to fight the stormbird? If Amira let her go now, how would she ever find her again?

Then there was Amira's mothers, looking at her with love and fear. Amira had never been away from them, had never navigated without them. But she understood, now, that this wasn't their voyage to take.

Amira knew what she needed to do.

She gave Leo a slight nod before she bent down, gripping the edge of the rowing boat. Her mothers reached out to pull her on. And Amira shoved, with all of her might. The waves dragged the rowing boat away with force as Leo leaped towards the dhow, Semek's bag swinging from his shoulder.

'Amira!' her mothers cried, desperately trying to row towards her.

Leo's hands barely grasped the edge of the dhow. The bottom half of his body dunked into the water, submerging his *jinni*. People scrambled past, too panicked to help, nearly crushing his fingers beneath their boots.

Amira scrambled to help Leo up, and took one last look at her mothers.

Jamila was sobbing, with Dunya holding her in her arms.

'Amira!' they cried.

'I love you,' Amira cried back, her voice shaking. And then, with Leo by her side, she launched into the crowd, in search of the girl with the lizard in her hair.

Everyone was running towards the bottom deck of the dhow while Amira and Leo fought against the current, all the way up. The smoke thickened as they reached the second level. The cages that had been filled with animals were now empty, and the last few people were fleeing.

The stall that had once held the love potions was scorched, the bottles of tonic smashed all around it. Amira realized then that's what had caused the fire. Magic without rules was dangerous. Her mothers had warned them of that.

Amira felt the ground beneath her shift. The dhow was sinking.

The stormbird launched itself at the dhow a second time, almost knocking it sideways. The dhow managed to right itself, but Amira knew it wouldn't take a third hit. She hoped her mothers were safely away by now. She tried to look past the railings in search of *Tigerheart*, but she couldn't see anything.

Amira coughed, smoke clogging her throat and nose.

It made her eyes stream. She covered her mouth and nose with her jacket.

'To the top,' Amira shouted to Leo, through gritted teeth. If she was wrong, and the lizard girl had escaped some other way, she could be leading them to their deaths.

Leo followed, Semek by his side.

When they reached the top deck of the midnight souk, Amira could breathe again. The stairs behind them were entirely engulfed by fire. She shut the door behind her, hoping to keep it at bay for as long as possible.

The only way they would get off the dhow now was to jump into the ocean, and it was a long way down. Amira tried not to think of their chances, or the people she had seen dragged under the waves.

Then Amira's eyes fell on the girl. She was standing at the edge of the railing, preparing to launch herself off the dhow like a bird.

'Wait!' screamed Amira. 'Wait!'

The girl turned towards them, eyes wide. Her lizard *jinni* buried itself in her hair.

'We have *jinn* too,' said Leo desperately, holding up Semek, his scales sparkling like jewels. 'Look.'

The girl stepped off the railing. She looked between Amira and Leo with suspicion, before resting her eyes on Semek. Something shifted in her face, and she nodded.

'We can't talk about this now. We have to get off the dhow,' she said. 'Don't worry – I have a way out.'

Amira and Leo had no other choice but to follow. Amira peered over the giant dhow's golden railings to see a piece of rope at the base of it, attached to a small dhow far below.

'Whose is that?' she asked.

'I stole it,' said the girl.

Amira recoiled. 'You're a *pirate?*' she said, spitting the word out like it tasted bitter.

The girl rolled her eyes. 'If that's what you want to call me.'

Amira didn't trust pirates, but what choice did she have?

'Use this,' said the girl, handing both Leo and Amira splintered pieces of wood. 'And watch me.' Without another word she placed the wood on top of the rope, held on to either side of it, and zip-lined off the dhow.

'I'll go next,' said Leo, a slight smile on his face. 'You had better not abandon me again.'

Amira laughed humourlessly, turning to see the fire peeking through the cracks in the door. 'It's either a pirate, or the fire.'

'If anyone can fight fire, it's you,' said Leo. And then he too launched himself off the dhow, Semek in tow.

As Amira took up her position at the railings, the door behind her burst open. A stream of fire shot towards her, like a hand. She jumped, and flew through the air, landing hard on the small dhow below. She tumbled on to the floor, knocking the wind out of her. When she looked back, the midnight souk was nothing but a ball of fire.

The stormbird returned to its nest.

The lizard girl was already rowing them away. Amira desperately searched for *Tigerheart* in the distance. She thought of her mothers, swept away into the darkness. She thought about all of the items found and traded at the souk, lost to the ocean once more.

Now she knew how many lives the stormbird could destroy.

Amira felt angry. Angrier than she had ever been. It was as if the fire from the dhow was raging inside her. This time she would let it out.

She let her anger drive her away from the burning dhow and towards an uncertain future. She wasn't going to let the stormbird win. Not again. She was going to fight it in the only way she knew how: with the anger that burned inside of her.

Chapter 25

You've done well to stick with me for so long. What a journey we've been on so far! Our young hero has got herself into quite the predicament, and it is only the beginning for her. You don't want to know what happens when . . . Well, I'll let you find out.

No peeking! It'll spoil the journey.

A story is a journey of sorts, don't you agree? While our characters run back and forth (and doesn't it seem quite tiring to you?) we sit here, cosy and warm, reading about it in the pages of a book. But that doesn't mean we haven't been on the journey with them. And that's the thing about journeys: they come in many different forms.

Some journeys are physical, others emotional; though most are both. Some would argue that emotional journeys are the most arduous of all. I would agree, having been on one myself.

You might be wondering who I am, and how I came to know these children and their stories. Have you any guesses? Am I the woman from the souk warning everyone of the stormbird? I imagine her stories would be terrifying indeed.

Or am I the woman in the rowing boat, guiding strangers to the souk, who trades stories for a living?

I can tell you one thing: I am neither.

I'll let you take a third guess. Go on.

I can't possibly tell you if that was correct, but I can promise that you'll find out by the end of this book. Let's get back to it, shall we? The sun will soon rise again, and we have a lot of ground (or should I say sea) to cover.

Chapter 26

'What is your name?' asked Amira, when they were safely away from the burning dhow and the waves had calmed once more.

The night had turned clear. The sky dipped into the sea like a paintbrush, the horizon fading into the darkness.

'Farah,' said the girl. 'And my *jinni* is called Layla.'

Layla tentatively peeked out of Farah's hair, and Amira could just about discern her teardrop-shaped head, black beady eyes and webbed feet. Her tail hung down, swooping over Farah's left ear, like a loose strand of hair.

Amira tried not to think about Namur, and the way his tail wrapped round her neck.

Once Amira and Leo had introduced themselves, the dhow fell silent. There were so many questions, so much to discover about one another, that it was difficult to know where to begin.

'How did you manage to steal the dhow?' asked Amira,

glancing around. It was small, much smaller than *Tigerheart*. Its paint was faded and worn, the sail dirty from the elements. They were seated, at the moment, on the top deck, which had a small hatch that led to the lower deck.

'I hid,' answered Farah. 'I'm good at that,' she said proudly.

'Why?'

It was Leo who asked the question this time. Amira saw he had a long gash down his arm. His face was covered in soot from the fire, and his voice croaked when he spoke.

'To get to the midnight souk,' Farah said simply.

'Why did you go to the midnight souk?' asked Leo.

'And what were you looking for?' added Amira.

'Who says I was looking for anything?' Farah countered. Layla returned to the depths of her hair.

'Why else would you go?' answered Amira.

Farah eyed Amira and Leo. Then she shook her head.

'*You* were the ones who found *me*. So you have to tell me what you know first.' She turned to Amira. 'He has a *jinni* and you don't.'

Farah's words stung, as if Amira had been slapped.

'I do have a *jinni*!' Amira snapped, louder than she had intended. 'Namur. He was taken,' she continued, her voice shaking.

Farah softened. Amira guessed she was thinking of her own lizard *jinni*. 'How?' she whispered.

'The stormbird,' Amira explained, and she told Farah what had happened the night she rowed out to sea.

Farah was looking at her strangely. 'Is your *jinni* a cat?' she asked, pulling something from her bag.

A brass bottle.

It resembled the one from the stories Amira's mothers had told. It was gilded, just small enough to fit in Amira's hands, with a pearl clasp.

'Yes.' Amira didn't take her eyes off the bottle. 'Why?'

Farah silently handed her the bottle. Amira felt it in her hands. It was warm, heavy and somehow familiar . . .

'Is this . . .' asked Amira, her voice wobbling, 'Namur?'

Farah nodded.

Amira tried to get into the bottle, prise the pearl clasp open. But it was stuck firm, as if wedged shut.

She began crying. Her tears turned to sobs. Leo pulled her in for a hug, though she barely felt it. Her body was fizzing, like the stormbird's current.

'H-how?' was all Amira managed to stutter at Farah.

'It's a long story,' Farah said. 'And one I'm not entirely sure you'll believe . . .'

But she cleared her throat, and she began to tell it.

The Tale of the Three Mermaid Sisters

Once a young girl and her lizard *jinni* set off on their very first adventure. It was an accidental adventure, but that's a story for another time. All I can say is that it was an exciting one, filled with the sorts of things you might expect from an adventure. Daring. Danger. And discoveries.

But it was an adventure filled with worry too. Lots of it.

Towards the end of their first adventure, the girl and her *jinni* embarked on a new one. They had been on the run, searching for somewhere to sleep.

They were walking along the coast, better to keep track of their path, when they heard singing from the sea. At first the girl and her lizard *jinni* thought it was the wind and carried on their way.

But then the singing grew louder. Songs of loss, of longing, of love.

And, eventually, the girl and her *jinni* stopped. They saw, glinting in the distance, three fishtails approach. Each tail was attached to the body of a woman.

Mermaids! The girl could hardly believe it. They weren't as she had expected – beautiful with lustrous hair. These mermaids were scaly, with sharp angles and even sharper teeth. But the girl trusted them. She could read their emotions, and she knew they were good.

'Hello, young one,' said the first of the three mermaids.

'Hello,' said the girl, her lizard *jinni* nuzzling into her hair. 'Your singing is beautiful.'

'Thank you,' said the second of the mermaids.

'My sisters and I have come to ask for your help,' said the third mermaid.

And she told a story of another girl who had saved them. The girl she spoke of was the very same age, and she had a *jinni* too, though hers was a cat.

'She was kind to us, long ago, when we had no one to help us. We were trapped in a lagoon, with no way to reach the ocean,' said the second mermaid.

'She saved us, gave us freedom and hope again,' the third mermaid finished.

'You see,' said the first mermaid, 'we live for hundreds and hundreds of years, and it can get rather dull when you only have a lagoon to swim in.'

'And no one to speak to,' said the second.

'We have loved life at sea,' said the third. 'We've made friends and seen all sorts of wonderful things . . .'

'But today we have a sad story,' said the first mermaid, interrupting the third.

'Very sad,' agreed the second.

The first mermaid continued. 'Our friend's *jinni* has been snatched . . .'

'By a great bird!' said the second. 'It looked like a roc.'

'But it wasn't,' added the third. 'We knew as much from its shining eyes.'

'We've no idea where it came from,' said the first. 'But there is a powerful current in the air around it.'

'I followed the bird,' added the third. The other two fell silent, allowing their sister to speak. 'After it snatched the *jinni*. I tried to reach its nest, where it lay to rest. But it sat at the horizon, and no matter how far I travelled, day and night, with no rest, or food . . .'

The second mermaid cleared her throat. 'Perhaps you

could tell a shorter version of the tale?'

The third mermaid scowled. 'It's easy for you to say. You were not the one who had to swim across an ocean to find the jinni. It is my story, and I'll tell it how I like.'

'Go on, sister,' said the first mermaid. 'Tell your story.'

The third sister huffed, lifting her chin high, and then she continued. She told a story of sharks to be fought, and dhows to be avoided. After a long, long tale of suffering, she finally came to the conclusion of her story.

'I realized then that I would never find the nest. And so I stopped trying. I was ready to return home, having failed my mission. But as I was swimming against the current, the way I often like to do, I saw something glint up ahead.'

The second mermaid swished her tail irritably. The first frowned at her, and she stopped.

'I reached down for it,' continued the third mermaid. 'And would you know it? It was a brass bottle. I felt a strange magic coming from it. The same kind of magic I had sensed from the girl who had saved our lives. And so I swam, faster than I have ever swum before . . .'

At this point in the story the mermaid became distracted by her adventures once more. She spoke of the stormbird's wrath as it chased her across the sea. But, eventually, she told of the moment she had reached her sisters again, and how they had pieced together the mystery. The stormbird had trapped the cat *jinni* in the brass bottle and dropped it in the ocean, never to be found.

'Except I *did* find it,' said the third mermaid proudly.

'But *how* did you find it?' the girl asked, entranced. 'It's like finding a single jewel in all of the desert!'

'Determination,' the third mermaid said. 'And perhaps . . . magic.'

'Mermaid magic,' clarified the second.

'Now it's time for our story,' said the first mermaid. 'While our sister . . . our *brave* sister,' she added hastily as the third mermaid scowled, 'was away, my sister and I pulled the girl to shore, ensuring her safety.'

'And once the three of us were reunited,' continued the second mermaid, 'we came up with a plan.'

They were all getting quite excited by their story. Though they had made friends at sea, they rarely had anyone to speak to. Fish were not big conversationalists, and they could only approach humans to grant a single favour, or if they were summoned by song.

'We have already saved the girl from the stormbird once. The rules of our magic are such that we cannot find her again.'

'That is why we have come to you,' said the first mermaid. 'You have a *jinni* too, so you understand.'

The girl and her lizard *jinni* did understand. They understood very well indeed.

'How can we help?' she asked.

'Well,' said the first mermaid, 'there will soon be a midnight souk . . .'

Chapter 27

'You pirated a dhow to find *me*?' said Amira. She was gripping Namur's bottle tight, as if she would never let it go.

Farah grinned. 'I said you would understand, once you knew.'

'You know how to navigate?' asked Amira, impressed.

Farah snorted. 'Not at all. The mermaids helped me.' She peered out at the ocean now, as if expecting them to rise up to the surface. 'But they've gone.'

'I wonder if the stormbird chased them away,' mused Leo.

Amira nodded. 'Perhaps.'

'So,' asked Farah, 'what do we do now?'

Amira gazed at her bottle, and thought back to the city of brass. Her mothers had gone there and released Namur the first time. Could she release him again?

Amira thought of her father too, and what it would

mean to see him . . .

'We're going to chart a course to an island,' she said, looking between Farah and Leo. 'And that's where we'll release my *jinni*.'

'After that,' continued Leo, catching on, 'we'll find a way to reach the stormbird. And stop it.'

'Wait,' said Farah, holding her hands out. 'You want to *go to* the stormbird? Didn't you see what happened at the midnight souk?'

Amira and Leo nodded.

'And didn't you hear what the mermaids said?'

Amira and Leo nodded again.

'And you *still* want to go?' Farah looked at them both as if they were mad. Then she shook her head. 'You can do that on your own. Just drop me on land and then –'

'I'm afraid we can't do that,' said Amira.

Farah looked between her and Leo, alarmed. 'Why not?' she asked. Her lizard *jinni* rustled in her hair, digging further into her nest of curls.

'It's my turn to tell a story now,' Amira said. And that's when she told Farah all about the city of brass.

Chapter 28

'Wow,' said Farah, when Amira finished her story. 'So this island is where *jinn* are from?'

'Yes!' said Amira. 'The stormbird, the roc in the middle of the table – it's connected to the *jinn* somehow. And that might be our key to stopping it.'

'Is that why you need me?' It seemed that Farah had already resigned herself to her third accidental adventure.

Amira nodded. 'What do you know about *jinn*? Leo and I have worked a few things out . . .'

She told Farah about her anger and Leo's nerves. She told her about the fizzing current, and their most important discovery of all: that the stormbird was connected not to just one human but to *everyone*, because it drank their emotions.

'And spat them back out, as a storm,' Amira finished.

Farah nodded, resolutely. 'I have to help. Especially if we're the only three moonchildren out there.'

Amira had never heard the word. 'Moon what?'

Farah laughed. 'It's a name I came up with because of the moon cycle. *Jinn* get their power from the moon. Didn't you know?'

'No,' said Amira, too curious to be embarrassed. 'How?'

'Well,' said Farah. 'I noticed it right before a new moon. My powers would get weaker.'

'And when the moon is full?' asked Leo. 'Do your powers get stronger too?'

'Yes!' said Farah. 'It's a small change, because I think the *jinn* store powers.'

'Like a battery!' said Leo excitedly, though Amira didn't know what that was.

She sat in silence for some time, soaking in this new information. It seemed, as soon as Amira thought she understood magic, it grew and spread and changed, like branches in a tree.

'Moonchild,' she said, testing the word out.

Leo was busy scribbling in his notebook. 'This all makes sense!' he said. 'It's why the stormbird rests before each attack. It uses up all of its power and has to recharge itself. I've been logging its movements, look. It always attacks for no more than an hour at a time, and rests for days. That's when the weather goes weird.'

'Do you think it's powered by the moon, too?' asked Amira.

'I'm not sure,' admitted Leo.

'Will the brass island be able to tell us?' asked Farah.

'I hope so,' said Leo. 'But how are we going to get there? Your mothers said they couldn't find it again, Amira.'

'I know,' Amira said. 'But Farah gave me an idea.'

Farah grinned. 'Glad to help. Could you remind me what I did . . .?'

'Mermaids!' said Amira. 'They helped you find the midnight souk, didn't they? If there were whispers of an island made of brass, they would know.'

She ran to the bow and leaned into the ocean, waiting to hear the mermaids sing. But they didn't.

'Where are they?' she asked. 'Where are you!' she screamed into the silence.

But all that met her were gentle waves lapping up against the side of the dhow, and the breaths of her crewmates beside her.

❖✦❖

The three moonchildren drifted aimlessly across the ocean, leaving the midnight souk far behind. Amira shouted and shouted, but the mermaids did not appear.

'Why won't they come?' asked Amira. She often cried when she felt frustrated, and she wiped her tears away unashamedly. 'I need their help.' She felt entirely lost. The mermaids had found her and Farah before, but this time *she* was supposed to find *them*.

'They won't come to me either,' said Farah, gently reminding Amira, 'because they've already granted us a favour.'

Leo stared into the distance, a peculiar expression on his face.

'My father once . . .' he said, letting the thought disappear like a puff of smoke. And then he parted his lips, and he sang.

It was a ballad Amira hadn't heard before; it called out to the ocean for help. When Leo had finished the song, Amira closed her eyes and imagined each note, like songbirds, flying across the ocean to find the mermaids.

Chapter 29

The night was silent. The three moonchildren waited for minutes, then hours. Eventually, tiredness took over and they settled beneath the stars to catch a few hours of sleep.

Just as Amira was drifting off, something stirred beneath the water.

'Look!' she said, waking Leo and Farah up.

At first it was just a ripple. Then three fins cut through the surface of the water, bringing a wave that rocked the dhow from side to side. And then three identical faces, but for the colour of their skin and hair, peered up at them with shining eyes. The mermaids resembled humans from the waist up, but instead of skin they had scales that shimmered in the moonlight, and eyes like fish.

'Hello, Amira,' said the first sister. 'So lovely to see you again.'

'Thank you,' said Amira in a rush, 'for finding my

jinni's bottle, and for saving me. I can't . . . I . . .'

'It's our honour,' said the second mermaid.

'It was me,' the third pointed out. 'I found the bottle by myself. I put myself in danger to –'

'So you did, dear sister,' interrupted the first mermaid. 'Now, who called us with that beautiful voice?'

'I did,' said Leo, shyly.

'How did you know to call us?' asked the second mermaid.

'My father.' Leo's face darkened as his mind wandered back to the past. 'He said that when you're lost at sea, if you sing, you will find your way. And, well, I remembered this song from long ago . . .'

The second mermaid nodded. 'It is our song – the mermaid's song, our calling.'

'So Leo,' said the first mermaid, 'what is it we can do for you?'

Leo looked at Amira and Farah. 'We want to find the brass island,' he said. 'To return the bottle, restore Amira's *jinni* and defeat the stormbird.'

The mermaids fell silent. It seemed, for the first time, they weren't sure what to say.

'We can't help you with that,' said the first mermaid at last. 'The brass island you speak of is centuries old. It was once the source of all magic in this world, but now it is cursed forever.'

'Cursed how?' asked Amira.

'Brass stops magic. Traps it. The way the bottle trapped your *jinni*.'

'But why was the island cursed? And who cursed it?' Amira persisted.

The mermaids had no answer.

'Why can't we find it?' Amira demanded in frustration. 'I can chart the stars, the sun, anything. I've been doing it all my life.'

The first mermaid smiled a little. 'Can you chart an ever-moving whale?'

Amira had never before navigated something moving. Islands stood still, waiting to be found. Even the midnight souk had a location. But whales . . . Amira and her friends might travel for years and years and never find what they were looking for.

'It's impossible,' said the third mermaid.

'It isn't,' said Amira at once. She wasn't giving up hope. Not now she had Namur's bottle in her grasp. 'If my mothers did it once, we can do it again.'

The first mermaid laughed. 'Sailors have driven themselves mad searching for it. They hope to find it, release the magic and take it for their own. Or else they expect to loot the island of brass and sell it on for riches.'

Leo shuffled uncomfortably. Amira remembered his story, and how his father had tried to find an ever-moving island filled with riches . . .

'Leo,' she began.

'I know,' Leo said. 'My father knew about it too.'

'Sailors are mad men,' continued the third mermaid

without tact. 'All of them.'

Leo flinched. Seeing his hurt ignited a fire within Amira.

'But I'm not a sailor,' she said with certainty. 'I'm a sea witch.'

'We must go now,' said the second mermaid some time later, once they had found out all they could. 'The storm is brewing once more, and it isn't safe.'

Clouds had formed around the stormbird's nest. It was gathering its strength, preparing for another attack. They had to find the island of brass before the stormbird found them.

The first mermaid turned to Leo. 'You never asked for your favour. When you're ready, call for us. We will return.'

'Thank you,' said Leo.

'And best of luck, sweet Amira,' said the second mermaid. 'We wish we could have helped you more.'

When they were gone, Amira slumped back down in the stolen dhow.

'What'll we do?' asked Farah.

Amira sighed. 'I'm not sure, but we have to do something.'

Farah's concern wrapped round them all. 'We don't have tools, and we're running out of food. Perhaps we should just –'

'No!' said Amira. 'I'm not giving up.' She would sail forever until she found the island. She would never give up, not until she freed Namur.

'Can you think of anything else from your mothers' story?' asked Farah. 'Something that'll give us a clue?'

The red haze from the blood moon threw a strange light on Leo and Farah. It was as if there was a great gash on Leo's face. It made Amira shiver. 'The blood moon,' she finally said. 'My mothers found the island during the blood moon. If *jinn* are from the brass island, and they get their power from the moon, then maybe the whale surfaces during the blood moon. Just like the midnight souk!' Amira wanted so much to grasp at any hope she could. But Farah pierced the bubble of excitement that had formed in her chest.

'We only have one more night of the blood moon,' she warned. 'And we still don't have a way to track a moving island.'

Something was nagging at Amira. Something she had

seen at the midnight souk. Then she remembered.

'There might be a way,' said Amira, feeling, for the first time, like the captain her mother had taught her to be. 'Let me explain.'

Chapter 30

'Whales can sing,' said Amira simply.

She had known this from stories her mothers had told her as a child, but the spell from the midnight souk had reminded her. *The whisper of a snake. The song of a whale. The cry of a newborn.*

Farah frowned. 'So why don't we ever hear them?'

'They don't sing like us,' explained Amira. 'They sing underwater. We just need a way to listen.'

'How?' asked Farah, peering into the ocean as if it might offer a solution.

It was Leo who answered. 'Amira, do you have the radio I gave you?'

'Yes!' said Amira. Reaching into her pouch, she pulled the radio out, red and shining. She handed it to Leo.

And it was as if she had given him her excitement too. He started muttering to himself, writing things down in his notebook, crossing other things out. He cleared his throat, ready to present his findings. 'We can use the radio to track the whale song.'

Amira and Farah were silent for a moment. Then Amira grinned.

'I knew you'd have an answer, Leo!' she said.

'We just need one more thing . . .' said Leo. 'Something none of those other sailors had before us.' He hopped from one side of the boat to the next and grabbed Semek. Amira couldn't help but think about how natural he seemed out here in the ocean. 'We can use the radio to listen to the whale song and find out how *far away* the whale is,' he explained. 'And then we'll use Semek as a compass to show us *which direction* to travel in.'

Next to his notes, Leo drew a diagram to show Amira and Farah what he meant. At one end of the diagram was the radio, attached to what looked like a funnel. At the other end was a device with lots of wires sticking out of it.

'This is the speaker,' Leo explained, pointing at the diagram. 'Once I change the wires around a bit, the speaker will play the whale song through the radio!'

'That,' said Amira, 'sounds like an impossible magic.'

'Not magic,' grinned Leo. 'Science. And with science anything is possible.'

◇❈◇

Spirits were high on the dhow, as everyone adapted to their new roles. Farah took over as lookout while Leo and Amira gathered everything they needed to make Leo's contraption.

'I have a spare speaker in here somewhere . . .' Leo said, rummaging through his bag of random objects. Amira saw the metal sphere he had shown her, wrapped up in a piece of cloth, as well his notebook, gloves and an assortment of tools. 'Ah! Here it is!' He pulled out a box bristling with colourful wires, and put on his gloves.

'What next?' asked Amira.

'A funnel.' Leo showed her what the funnel needed to look like, using a piece of paper. 'I'll start working on the rest of it while you search.'

Amira began rummaging around the lower deck of the dhow. It was cramped down here, barely the size of her cabin back home on *Tigerheart*, and she had to hop over Leo and wriggle around his contraption on the floor. She had Namur's bottle tucked into her belt, so he never left her side. And she wondered, for a moment, whether being trapped in the bottle was like walking around this cabin. Was Namur in his cat form? Or was he invisible, a caged spirit? Did he sense that she was near?

The room was a mess, boxes and crates stacked into a corner and half emptied on to the floor. There were nets, and fishing wire, and empty glass bottles, but nothing that looked like a funnel.

Every so often Amira stopped her search to watch Leo. Science, she thought, was complicated. Reading emotions, mixing tonics, telling fortunes – they all seemed easy in comparison to Leo's task.

'Found it yet?' Leo asked, peering up at her.

Amira returned quickly to her search. Her panic was growing. What if she couldn't find what Leo needed? What then?

Her eyes fell on the empty glass bottles again. She picked a bottle up and inspected the bottom. Then, she turned to one of the crates, lifted the bottle in the air and smashed it down.

Glass shattered. Leo screamed, and Amira covered her face.

'Everything OK down here?' asked Farah, peeking her head through the porthole. Her eyes fell on Amira, who was wielding the broken bottle like a weapon. 'Had enough of us, have you?' she joked.

'Will this do?' Amira asked Leo as Farah vanished again.

Leo inspected it. 'No,' he eventually said.

'Well, I don't know what else to do!' Amira snapped, throwing her arms up.

Leo laughed. 'I meant, *that* bottle isn't right. You need a wider one. Like this.' He held another bottle up to show her. 'Try again.'

Amira held the wider bottle aloft, then smashed it down. 'That felt good,' she admitted, handing the broken bottle to Leo with a grin.

They were closer than ever to getting Namur back. Amira couldn't wait. She was so used to his weight on her shoulders that she felt unbalanced without him. And – strangest of all – she couldn't read anyone's feelings, not in the way she was used to.

'What do you think of Farah?' Amira asked Leo, lowering her voice to a whisper.

'She's nice,' Leo said, making some adjustments to the radio and the glass funnel. 'She helped us.'

'But she's hiding something,' Amira pointed out. 'And I think that's weird. We don't even know what her emotion is. Look at me and you. I'm angry outside *and* inside.'

'I know,' said Leo, chuckling.

Amira scowled at him. 'And *you*,' she said. 'You're a nervous mess all the time.'

'What exactly is your point?'

Amira bit her lip. Had she gone too far? Probably.

She crouched down, lowering her voice to a whisper again. 'I have no idea how Farah's really feeling, because she doesn't *show* it.'

'Why don't you just ask her, then?'

'I . . .'

'That's how you get to know people,' Leo said. 'You show an interest in them and ask nicely. You don't have to spy on their emotions.'

'But if you *were* to read her emotions . . .'

Leo stopped what he was doing. 'She's going through something at the moment,' he said at last. 'I can't tell what, but it makes her feel sad. Be nice to her.'

'I *am* nice!' said Amira petulantly. Why did everyone always say that to her?

She sulked in the corner for a few minutes, before Leo nudged her and she was forced to look at him.

'It's ready,' he said, his face flushed. 'Shall we test it out?'

◇ ✦ ◇

Up on the deck the sun had just begun to rise and the moon waved goodbye for the day.

The group huddled at the bow together. Leo slipped Amira's glass funnel into the water and pulled the radio towards them.

Everything was silent apart from the lapping of the ocean waves and the occasional sound of Layla scuttling in Farah's hair.

'What's supposed to happen?' asked Amira.

'Shhh!' said Leo. 'Wait.'

The three moonchildren huddled over the radio, listening until their limbs were stiff.

'There it is!' said Leo suddenly. 'Can you hear it?'

At first all Amira could hear was the sound of rushing

water. She closed her eyes and remembered what it was like to sail without worries. Then, faintly, she heard a cry in the distance. It was a little scratchy, but unmistakable.

'Is that –' she said, the words catching in her chest. 'Is that the whale? *Our* whale?'

'Yes!' said Leo. 'There can't be many others in the Sahar Peninsula.'

'It's beautiful!' said Farah.

The whale song was unlike anything Amira had heard before. She thought birdsong was lovely, but this was better. It was as if the sea had a ballad of its own.

'The closer we get,' Leo explained, 'the louder its song will be. That's what the funnel is for.'

'Shall we start charting?' asked Farah.

Leo's smile slipped. He peered into Semek's bowl, which he had placed at the edge of the dhow. 'It's finally time for you to play your part, Semek,' he said to his *jinni*. 'It's time for you to be our compass.' His hands shook as he lifted Semek out.

Amira put a hand on his arm. 'Are you sure, Leo?'

Leo nodded, though his jaw was tight. 'It's silly. He'll be right beside us. It's just . . .'

'I know,' said Amira.

'It's very brave of you to let him go,' said Farah from Amira's other side. Layla had crawled from her hair down her arm and wrapped herself round her wrist. Perhaps the *jinni* was beginning to trust them.

The three moonchildren stared into the sunrise as Leo placed Semek into the ocean. They could see Semek's tiny golden fins gleaming, as he lapped at the water for a moment. He looked like a beacon of light guiding them. Then his body spun, like the point of a compass, until he stopped, nose forward, and started swimming.

'That's east!' said Amira. 'We sail east.'

And she gathered her crew as they began to chart the island on the back of a whale.

Chapter 31

The next night – the last night of the blood moon – was clear, and the waves were as smooth as silk as the three moonchildren raced to the city of brass.

While Leo navigated, passing instructions to Amira at the wheel, Amira instructed Farah to adjust the sail. They danced around each other, each of them focused on their tasks for hours and hours until the moon was full and high.

'Where did you learn to navigate?' Farah asked Amira.

'My mother,' said Amira, and she told Farah about Dunya and how she'd taught Amira to read maps before she could read words. 'I want to be like her some day.'

Farah smiled. 'I haven't met her, so I can't be sure, but I think you already are.'

Amira's heart soared at Farah's words. She thought of Leo's advice. 'If you ever need to talk to someone,' she said awkwardly, 'about, uh, anything, I'm here.'

Farah nodded. 'Thank you.'

In the distance the stormbird began to stir. It only served to push Amira harder. She clung to the heavy wheel, guiding the dhow until her arms were sore.

Hours passed. The group fell silent, focused only on

their tasks. Leo's neck ached from bending down to navigate. Farah's hands were blistered, the way Amira's had been when she had first learned to work with rope. Amira carried the weight of her crew the way Dunya had for years.

'Want some food?' Farah held out a sack of dates.

'Where did you get these?' Amira asked, stuffing several whole dates into her mouth.

Leo grabbed a few and returned to his spot by the bow. It seemed he didn't want to leave Semek alone.

'I stole them,' said Farah, shamefaced. 'They were on the side of a cart. I was hungry.'

'I stole a fish once,' said Amira, thinking back to the first evening at the port. 'Well, Namur did.'

'I can't wait to meet him,' said Farah. 'He sounds wonderful.'

Amira felt a sudden jolt of nerves. She touched the brass bottle at her belt. What if Namur was mad at her? What if he didn't want to be her *jinni* any more?

She shook the thought aside. 'When does your *jinni* show itself, Farah?' she asked.

Layla, who had been asleep in Farah's hair, crawled out

of her nest, peering up at Amira with big bug eyes that shone in the darkness. She stuck her forked tongue out three times, before nestling back inside.

'When I'm feeling curious,' said Farah.

Amira raised her eyebrows. 'You don't seem curious at all.'

Farah shrugged. 'Some feelings are easier to hide than others,' she said. She looked at Amira, and smiled.

'What?' asked Amira, suddenly shy.

'I can *see* your anger,' said Farah. 'It's right there, at the surface. Like you're made of fire.'

Amira laughed. 'My mother says that –' she began. She stopped as her mind drifted towards Jamila, and how they fought, but laughed together too. She missed her mothers so much that she wasn't sure her heart could take it.

'I know how you're feeling right now,' said Farah.

'Really?' asked Amira, sniffing.

'Remember how the mermaids granted me a favour? Well, I asked them to send a message to my sister,' Farah said, looking away. 'So she would know that I'm safe.'

'You have a sister?' asked Amira.

Farah nodded, smiling a little. 'She's a troublemaker.

Always asking questions.'

Amira grinned. 'She sounds like the best sister.'

'She is,' Farah said. 'I miss her.'

'How did the mermaids find your sister to give them the message?'

'Their roc, the one they raised. The one you delivered them.'

'Where is your family? Where is your home?'

'That's a long story . . .' said Farah, going quiet. She turned away now, her attention on the sail again. Friendships, Amira realized, took time to build. Like a dhow. And she would have to learn to be patient.

◦ ✦ ◦

'The whale is getting closer!' said Leo some hours later. 'It's swimming towards us.'

'That means we should be able to reach it by midnight,' Amira said, 'judging by the moon's position in the sky. Why don't you rest?' she suggested to Farah, Jamila's advice swimming through her mind: *All great adventures begin with a nap.* 'We'll take it in turns.'

They would, after all, need all the strength they could muster to face the stormbird.

Farah crawled through the hatch, heading for the cabin. Amira focused her attention back to the sea. She thought of her mothers, and she hoped they had made it safely back to *Tigerheart*. She hoped Dunya would be proud of her for steering the dhow, and Jamila would approve of the way she was taking charge.

When it was her turn to rest, Amira fell back on to the old rag bed below deck and drifted off within seconds. But it only felt like she had been asleep for a few minutes before Farah came rushing down.

'Amira!' she said. 'We need you!'

The waves had grown choppier, angrier. The stormbird cried, and the sound of thunder and lightning followed. It flapped its wings, sending a great gust of wind that threatened to push them off course.

Blinking sleep from her eyes, Amira rushed to the wheel, desperately grasping at the spokes. 'We're so close!' she said through gritted teeth, wrestling with the wheel. 'So . . . close . . .'

'What do we do, Amira?' cried Farah.

Amira led her crew, like any good captain would.

She ordered Leo to keep listening for the whale, while

she held fast to the wheel and Farah brought the sail down. 'The mast will snap if we keep it the way it is,' she explained.

'Amira!' shouted Leo. 'Something's wrong . . .'

Dropping the wheel so it spun round, and round, and round, Amira scrambled over to where Leo was holding the radio. 'What now?' she said, frustration washing over her.

'It's stopped,' said Leo. 'The whale song. I don't know why.'

A fountain of water suddenly shot straight up from the waves ahead of them. Leo screamed and fell back on to Amira, knocking her in the chin. Pain shot up her jaw.

'What was that?' asked Leo, trembling.

Rubbing her chin, Amira leaned into the churning water and scooped a glimmering Semek up into his bowl. Her weight tipped the dhow forward.

A shadow rose from beneath the surface of the ocean, so large Amira couldn't see beyond it. The water parted. The dhow rumbled like they were caught in an earthquake.

Amira and Leo exchanged a look, and they knew.

Amira grabbed a rope, tying it round herself and her

friends. Then she tied them all to the mast, just like she had with the animals on *Tigerheart* the day the storm had come.

'Brace yourselves,' said Amira.

'What's happening?' asked Farah, looking scared.

'The whale,' Amira said. 'It's surfacing.'

Chapter 32

All around them, the ocean glinted and shone, like a million pearls were gathering, waiting to be plucked.

The spire of a building shot up from the water first, followed closely by dozens of other spires and turrets all coated in brass. Water cascaded down the sides of the rising buildings, forming waterfalls that pooled together. Brass palm trees rose next, followed by brass animals and brass people.

Something pushed hard against the bottom of the dhow, launching it into the air like a shooting star.

Armia's stomach churned and her body shook. 'Keep still!' she shouted at Farah and Leo.

'What's happening?' screamed Farah, Layla clinging to her hair.

The dhow groaned, and the wood splintered. 'We've landed on something,' Amira cried, trying to peer over the railing. 'A building, or a tree.'

Something smashed into the deck beneath them as wood collided with brass. But Amira wasn't afraid. She had been born here, after all.

'Wait for my instruction,' said Amira, like the captain she was.

Checking Namur's bottle was still safely tucked into her belt, she untied herself and crawled to the bow, as nimble as a cat. She chanced a look down. She was right: their dhow was perched on a tree. She had to work to stay balanced, so as not to tip it over.

Just beneath the tree was the statue of the guard and the horse that Jamila had described. And ahead was the city of brass, lighting up the ocean beneath the inky sky.

Every inch of the island was layered with algae. Each building, each tree was dripping with water, and the air smelled like salt and fresh seaweed.

'You can untie yourselves now,' said Amira, looking back at the others. 'But move slowly.'

Leo joined her first, then Farah. They all peered at the wall that surrounded the city, and at the houses that clustered together, spreading further apart as they led up to a grand palace.

The palace sat at the centre of the island, with a rounded roof tapering to a sharp point. And every single part of the structure was made of brass: the walls, the doors, even the windows.

Amira itched to climb down, to see the palace up close.

'That's where we need to go,' she said.

In the distance the stormbird watched. Its eyes, piercing the darkness, were drawn to the city of brass like a moth to a flame.

Chapter 33

'We can't touch anything,' warned Amira. She thought about her mother turning to brass; how, once, *she* had been coated in brass herself. Beneath them, the dhow shifted and groaned, threatening to fall off its perch in the tree.

'Then how are supposed to climb down?' asked Farah, anxiously peering over the edge of the dhow.

'With these!' said Leo, holding up his gloved hands. Amira noticed he had been wearing them a lot more on the little dhow. And she noticed he preferred to sleep above deck, which was cleaner than the raggedy old bed in the damp cabin.

'Perfect!' Amira said. 'I think I have a plan . . .'

Since he had the gloves, it was Leo's job to tie the rope round one of the stiff brass leaves on the tree. Amira showed him the best knots to use to make sure it was secure.

'I'll climb down first,' said Amira. 'Watch me closely and follow.'

Amira held on tight to the rope with both hands and stepped off the dhow on to the brass leaves. Then she bent her knees, testing the firmness beneath her feet, and jumped, releasing the rope as she went. When she landed again, on the trunk of the tree this time, she wobbled a little. Namur's bottle felt warm against her waist.

Amira bent her knees again, jumped and landed. Her feet slipped a little on the smooth brass tree trunk. She was used to climbing down the dhow in this way to clean it, but brass was slippier than wood.

It was hot and sweat poured down Amira's face as she concentrated on each step, each movement.

Three more jumps and Amira landed on the ground. Brass chimed beneath her boots.

'Now it's your turn!' she called up to Leo and Farah.

Leo climbed down next, though it took him longer than Amira. Semek's bowl swung from his shoulder, safely held in the rope bag that Amira had made, sloshing water over the side. But the *jinni* was safe. Then it was Farah's turn.

'That's good!' said Amira, as Farah climbed past the overhanging leaves.

But then the dhow began to wobble and slide off the brass fronds high above them.

'Run!' Amira grabbed Leo and pulled him to safety. She heard a crash behind her. Something struck her from behind, knocking her to the floor.

Amira's instinct was to put her hands forward, but she had nothing to protect them. So she rolled, landing back on her feet in one motion. Leo landed less gracefully, but his gloves had saved him.

'Farah?' Amira called, peering past the rubble of the dhow. 'Farah!'

'I'm OK,' Farah said weakly. She pushed herself up, placing her bare hands on the ground.

'Farah, no!' said Amira, but it was too late. By the time Farah pulled her hand away, it was coated in brass.

Mindless with fear, Amira rushed towards Farah. But she paused as Layla crawled out of Farah's hair. The lizard *jinni* skated down Farah's arm to where the brass had already begun to work its way up Farah's fingers, and licked Farah's coated skin with her forked tongue, the way Namur had with Amira all those years ago.

When Layla was finished, the brass had disappeared entirely. The lizard *jinni* scuttled back up to her nest.

'Well, that was lucky,' said Farah, shakily.

'How are we going to get off the island now?' Leo asked, gazing at the wreckage of the dhow.

'I don't know,' said Amira truthfully. 'We'll deal with that when it's time.'

It had taken them too long to get off the dhow. If they were right about the island and the blood moon, the whale would submerge at sunrise. And if that happened, they would be stranded in the middle of the ocean. Or drowned.

They had a lot to do before morning.

'Come on,' said Amira, barely giving Leo or Farah time to recover. 'Let's head towards the palace.'

'This is like being in a story,' said Farah, as they walked through the city gates into the souk. They peered through doorways and down alleyways;they watched people mid-chatter, going about their day.

Amira shuddered. This was her island. It was where she was from. If Namur hadn't freed her, she would be just like the rest of them. She closed her eyes and imagined what her life would have been like if the island hadn't been cursed. Would she have gone to school, like Leo? Would her father have taught her magic the way Dunya and Jamila had? Would Namur still have been her *jinni*?

The possibilities were endless, each like a door to a different life.

The group approached the palace moat that Dunya had described in the story, which was filled with gently rippling sea water. They crossed a brass bridge, crept through the open doors of the palace, and moved among the people queuing up to meet the king. Amira studied the brass walls Dunya had described, brushing away the algae with her sleeve.

Windows lined the walls too, from floor to ceiling. Once they would have been made of glass, but they were now all brass, like everything else. A brass staircase wound up to their right, like the mast of a dhow.

Something squirmed uncomfortably inside Amira as they walked through the palace in silence. Feelings she didn't quite understand.

Other people's feelings were a bit like reading the pages

of a book. Some of the words might be faded, or the pages torn and half missing, but they were there to be read nonetheless. Without Namur Amira's own feelings were like a book written in a language she did not recognize.

When they walked down the hall, their footsteps echoing in the silence, and slipped into the throne room, Amira finally understood why she felt so strange

There, perched on the throne, sat her father.

His arms were clasped together, as if holding something precious. A baby. But Amira wasn't a baby any more. She was twelve, and much too big to fit in his arms now.

She rushed to him and gazed into his eyes. They were her own, she could see that, even through the brass. His brow was slightly arched, like hers, and his nose was pointed. Amira reached for him, tears streaming down her face, but Leo gently pulled her back. Taking off his gloves, he handed them to her.

'Thank you,' said Amira, slipping the gloves on. And she reached out to hold her father's hand in hers.

As she did, she thought of her mothers. How Dunya had held her when she fell and scraped her knees on the dhow; how Jamila had spent hours teaching her to tie knots; and how they all shared stories together.

Her father had given her life, but her mothers had given her the world.

Eventually, Amira pulled away from her father and faced the round table. She saw Semek and Layla's brass bottles, where Dunya had left them. Namur's bottle was missing, because it was tied to Amira's belt. And right at the centre of the table was the stormbird, larger than all the others.

Amira's mothers had been wrong about one part of their story.

The table didn't resemble a clock face at all. It was clear to Amira, upon peering into the gaps, that they represented a different phase of the moon. And the stormbird, at the centre, was the sun.

'Look!' Leo said suddenly, inspecting the side of the table where intricate Arabic lettering wound round itself like vines. 'It's a story. The story of the *jinn* . . . and the stormbird!'

Amira bent down, cleared her throat, and read the story aloud.

The Tale of the King and
the Curse of Alhitan

There was an island called Alhitan, and it was the source of all magic in the Sahar Peninsula.

It was an island like many others. There were souks and schools, a palace and a king. But there was one thing that set Alhitan apart.

It was ever moving, because it stood on the back of a whale.

Those who lived on the other islands in the Sahar Peninsula frowned on the inhabitants of Alhitan. They disliked the *jinn* who roamed with them, encouraging people to feel their emotions in their purest form.

Emotions were, after all, the essence of magic. The more powerful the emotion, the stronger the magic. And magic, according to those in the Sahar Peninsula, was dangerous.

The people of the Sahar Peninsula also detested the stories shared by those who lived in Alhitan. Stories of love, and courage, of fighting for good over bad. These stories spread like wildfire, and the people wanted more. They wanted to feel and speak, and think for themselves, just like the people of Alhitan.

But the advisors of the Sahar Peninsula were afraid. They were afraid of losing their power, but they told the people that they were afraid of chaos, of the danger of unchecked emotion.

The people believed them. And they declared war. They knew that magic could be stopped in one way only: with brass.

They spent months, years, preparing for an attack on Alhitan. Then they sailed with one thousand dhows, all filled with molten brass. And with catapults bolted to the decks of the dhows, they hurled the molten metal at the island.

The king had known what would happen. He had heard whispers. And so he had made preparations. He placed eight *jinn* in brass bottles, holding them safe, hoping for the chance to release them back into the world one day to spread the freedom of emotions once more. And he wrote a story of his own, so that those who chanced upon his cursed island would learn of the sacrifice the people of Alhitan had made for magic.

And he protected his daughter.

This was his most important task. The king had lost his wife to illness, and his daughter was ever-more precious to him. A jewel.

Before placing them inside the bottles of brass, the king spoke to the *jinn* on the island. He asked for a *jinni* to seek his daughter once it was freed, and release her from her brass prison so she could grow and spread magic once again.

And finally the king declared that if Alhitan were destroyed, a great bird would hatch, and unleash all of the rage, grief, hatred and sadness on to the Sahar Peninsula. Every emotion held in by every person in every place but Alhitan. Emotions locked away for a thousand years.

In order to stop the bird all of the *jinn* would have to be released to spread their emotions to the world. And their bottles, then empty, would be used to trap the stormbird at its nest, until the people of the world were ready to feel freely once more.

When the advisors of the Sahar Peninsula launched

their weapons, the king went about his day as normal. He didn't warn his people. He wanted them to be at peace. He didn't fight back. He wanted the world to know that magic wasn't dangerous. True danger lurked in the lies of greedy men and the apathy of those who followed them without question.

And the king made sure, when the brass finally took him, that he was laughing: a lasting image of the joy that Alhitan brought to those who lived there.

The advisors of the Sahar Peninsula could not have foreseen the consequences of their actions. With the *jinn* trapped, and the island forced to the depths of the ocean, the stories of Alhitan ceased. Without stories, and *jinn*, people stopped thinking freely, stopped feeling freely.

But the emotions had to go somewhere . . .

Chapter 34

When Amira finished telling the story, her voice was shaking.

'The storm is my father's fault,' she said, feeling ashamed of him. She thought of all the houses destroyed by the storm, and all of the lives lost at the midnight souk. 'How could he do such a terrible thing? Why didn't he let his people leave the island and save themselves?' Amira cried. 'Why did he let his people turn to brass?'

'Where would they have gone?' Farah was teary-eyed, her lips quivering. 'I had to leave home because of my *jinni*. I had nowhere to go.'

And then Farah finally shared her story.

The First Accidental Adventure of Farah, the Moonchild

A year ago now, Farah had started a new school. Layla had gone with her. The other children were curious and had asked why she had a lizard in her hair. Farah had explained that Layla was her *jinni*.

Word spread that Farah was magical. The teachers ordered her to leave Layla at home, to renounce her magic, but she wouldn't. Instead, she tied her hair into a nest and snuck her lizard *jinni* into school in secret.

But one day one of the children told on Farah.

That night, an official knocked on Farah's door and demanded Layla. They would take her away and destroy her, because magic was dangerous and everyone knew it. Farah couldn't let that happen. She wouldn't. But if she didn't, they would burn her house down.

And so she climbed out of her window and hid in

a bush while the officials searched for her. She heard them smash the furniture in her room when they couldn't find her, and she saw her little sister peer at her from the window.

'Come back,' said her sister.

Farah pulled her sister in for a hug. 'I will,' she said. 'One day.' And then, she disappeared into the night, her sister's doleful eyes following her into the desert.

Chapter 35

'I walked for days and days without food and water,' Farah told Amira and Leo. 'I nearly didn't make it. Until I met the sea. I hadn't seen the sea before, didn't understand it. But port towns are busy and I managed to steal food and find corners to sleep in. That's when I met the mermaids.'

She finished her story with a shrug. 'So, if you're wondering why your father didn't let his people leave, perhaps it was because he knew they wouldn't have a life elsewhere.'

Amira realized, in that moment, that everyone had their own story. Hers was about finding Namur and defeating the stormbird, but Leo had his father and mother to worry about, and Farah had her sister, left behind. And all of their stories were far from over.

'I'm sorry, Farah,' she said simply, though she knew it wasn't enough. 'I promise you now I'll help you return home to your family.'

Farah wiped her eyes. 'Let's sort out the stormbird first, shall we?'

Amira thought about the magic that had leaked into the world: through her mothers, through her *jinni*. How it was forced to stay hidden, appearing only in the moonlight. And she thought of how stories were kept close, not to be shared.

But after today she would make sure magic would be seen, emotions felt, and stories shared all over the Sahar Peninsula.

Amira pulled Namur's bottle from her belt and placed it at the head of the table.

Just as her mothers had described, a silver light shot into the air. It formed, slowly, the body of a cat. Amira's body hummed with magic and her heart beat faster as she watched Namur.

Namur landed on the table – his body glowing bright, like the moon – and leaped, in one swoop, into Amira's arms. He nuzzled into her neck, tickling her with his whiskers, and purred louder than she had ever heard.

It felt to Amira like she had woken up from a dream. Everything before had been hazy and dull, but now . . . Now she was alive. The colours in the world were sharper, and the sounds louder. It was as if a wave had washed over her, stripping away the sadness she had felt since Namur had disappeared.

'I'm never letting you go again,' Amira told her *jinni*.

When they had finished embracing, Namur blinked at Leo and Semek, as if thanking them.

But before they had the chance to plan their next steps, the stormbird let out a strangled cry, and the ceiling rang like a bell as something landed hard on top of it.

'We need the other bottles!' Amira said at once. 'Once all the *jinn* are released, we can carry the bottles up to the roof and trap the stormbird.'

'So pretty simple, then?' said Farah sarcastically.

'Spread out,' ordered Amira, feeling stronger than she had in days. 'And put the bottles into the gaps as soon as you find them. But remember, don't touch anything.'

She quickly found the bag Dunya had dropped many moons ago, but it was empty now. The rest of the bottles had rolled out of it over the years.

The three moonchildren and their *jinn* set to work restoring the bottles. Each bottle shot out a jet of silver light. Amira watched as the *jinn* emerged and scattered in search of their humans. There was a fox, a mouse and a snake. Next there was a deer, with only one left to find.

'Where's the last one?' asked Farah.

Something had changed in the room. With each bottle restored the brass began to pull away, as the curse was lifted. Tiled ceilings in delicate patterns revealed themselves, as did colourful glass windows, and wooden tables and chairs.

But the ceiling was beginning to cave in as the stormbird pecked at the palace roof. Brass broke away from the walls. Sapphire gems and pearl carvings glinted at them, broken but perfectly preserved.

Tiles crumbled into little pieces. Windows shattered.

'The stormbird is going to break inside!' screamed Farah. 'And we don't have all of the bottles!'

Amira turned to her father, hoping he could offer her one last piece of wisdom.

Chapter 36

That's when Amira saw it. The final bottle, tucked beneath her father's throne.

Namur hopped down from her shoulders, and rolled it towards her.

She picked it up and looked into her father's eyes. The brass was beginning to peel away from them, and she could have sworn she saw him blink. It peeled away from his hands too, revealing an emerald-green ring, the same colour as Namur's eyes. She understood then what her father had done.

He wasn't allowing his people to be cursed; he was saving them. Rather than fight and lose lives, he chose to wait, to be patient. He knew Amira would free his people one day, and they would continue their lives together in Alhitan.

'Hurry, Amira!' yelled Leo.

Just as Amira was about to step towards her father, the

roof fell in, smashing into his throne. The king's brass body crumbled, shattering into pieces. The throne sat empty, as if welcoming her.

Amira fell silent, the shock rolling through her body in waves. For one brief moment she had a father. She had a new path to choose, like discovering an unknown island on a map. But the stormbird had taken it away from her, leaving behind her father's emerald ring, which rolled to her feet.

Amira bent down and picked it up, putting it on her gloved fingers. It was warm from her father's skin, too big for her. Amira may not have been able to free him, but she wanted something to remember him by. She would remember his sacrifice, his patience, and wear it like a cloak of protection.

Amira placed the final bottle into the table. A falcon.

It flapped its powerful wings several times, sending a gust of wind towards Amira. Then it swooped out of one of the open windows.

Leo gathered the empty bottles into Dunya's bag, while Farah waved at them from an open door. It was time for the final part of their journey.

Amira took the lead, Namur by her side. A winding staircase led them to the top of one of the four towers she had seen. It looked out to sea, towards the stormbird's empty nest.

The stormbird's red-and-orange tail swept down over the edge of the palace roof. Judging by its tail feathers, a single claw must have been the size of the dhow.

The air smelled of fire mingled with something else, like oranges. Amira couldn't tell where it was coming from.

'We need to get up to the roof!' she said.

'There's no way,' said Farah. 'This is the highest we can go.'

The brass curse was pulling away slowly, revealing the green of the land that surrounded them. The group now stood on an orange balcony, diamond-shaped patterns carved into it, edged in pearl. Soon the people on the island would be free too, and at the mercy of the stormbird.

'What if we lured the stormbird towards the rocks?' said Amira urgently. 'Leo, what do you think?'

She turned to Leo, but he was gone. On the floor lay Semek's bowl. The fish darted around in a panic, his eyes searching. And in that moment Amira knew. The fire and orange she had smelled moments before was the scent of determination, and it was coming from Leo.

He had taken Dunya's bag of bottles, leaving his own bag behind.

'Leo's gone!' said Amira, her voice shaking. 'He's going to lure the stormbird by himself. Keep his bag safe. And distract the stormbird.'

Farah found a guard, still made of brass, with a sword at its belt. 'Will this do?' she asked, unsheathing the sword. Now that the curse was lifting, she was able to touch the brass safely.

'Perfect,' said Amira. She swept Semek up and rushed back down the stairs to find Leo, Namur following like a shadow. And she ran out of the palace doors, a stitch building in her stomach, in desperate search of Leo.

It was raining heavily now and Amira couldn't see very well. Straight ahead of her, she found Leo's notebook, discarded on the floor. She picked it up, and studied the wet pages in confusion.

Leo had drawn a diagram of the stormbird's nest. Next to it, he wrote: *Trap the stormbird at its nest.* Amira realized this came from the story they had just read in the throne room. Then he wrote: *Can't reach nest. Unless*

But the writing had stopped.

Amira knew the nest was impossible to get to, sitting as it did at the horizon. How could they reach it there? Not even the mermaids could manage that.

And that's when she understood Leo's plan.

Rain dripped down from Amira's hair on to her face and clothes. Namur clung to her, keeping her warm and safe. She ran to the edge of the island, where the waves beat against the shore.

And there she heard Leo singing the mermaids' song.

Amira stopped at the rocks that fringed the shore. They were slippery in the rain, though the brass was beginning to peel away.

'Leo!' she cried, waving at him.

Leo was speaking to the mermaids. They turned from him to Amira and frowned.

Semek was swimming in his bowl in frantic swirls. 'Don't worry,' said Amira. 'We'll get him back!' But she was worried. She had never seen Leo look like this before.

Namur placed a paw on Semek's bowl, as if to comfort him.

'Leo!' Amira said, finally catching up with him. She was out of breath, panting. 'Leo, why didn't you tell us your plan?'

She expected to see Leo looking nervous, even scared. But he was smiling.

'Leo?' she said again, uncertain, holding out Semek's bowl.

'Ever since I met you, Amira, you made me feel like

I can go on adventures and see the world,' Leo said.

'You can!' Amira declared passionately. 'You're part of our family now, aren't you? We'll find the dhow and we'll sail all around. I'll show you the island of rocs and we – *Please!*'

Just as the sun kissed the horizon, and the night faded away, Leo held out his arms to hug Amira.

Relief washed over Amira as she pulled him towards her. Maybe he had changed his mind.

The ground beneath them began to shake.

'The island is going to sink,' she begged. 'We have to go now. We'll find another way to get to the nest. There has to be another way.'

Leo shook his head. 'There isn't,' he said. And, for a brief moment, he looked afraid.

'How do you know?' asked Amira.

'Science,' said Leo, as if that one word held all the answers.

The whale began to slide back into the ocean. The water was up to their ankles now. Farah joined them at the shore.

'We have to leave!' she panted, Layla nuzzled into her hair, shivering. 'The mermaids . . .'

Amira knew the people of Alhitan would be safe once the whale had submerged. Their magic would protect them. But what about the stormbird? What would it do now the curse was lifted? They had to leave, had to stop it.

Amira nodded. 'Let's go!' she said. 'The mermaids will keep us afloat, and we can wait for the stormbird's next attack.'

But Leo stepped back, and he looked up to the sky.

Amira followed his line of sight.

The stormbird was flying towards them, claws outstretched.

Leo looked between Amira and Semek. 'Will you keep him safe for me?' he asked.

Before Amira could respond Leo pushed her and Farah into the ocean.

Amira didn't close her eyes as she sank into the water. She kicked desperately towards the surface, towards the light.

She watched as the stormbird snatched Leo, the way a child might grab a sweet. And she saw them fly, fly, fly towards the horizon.

Strong arms pulled Amira away from the whale, and

she floated listlessly at the ocean's surface.

'Leo!' she screamed, watching the stormbird carry him to the horizon. 'Leo!' But it was no use. He was gone.

The stormbird landed, just as the sun rose full in the sky.

And then something changed. Like a cloud that had been pushed aside in the wind, the stormbird began to fade. Its nest disappeared too, until there was nothing but the straight line of the horizon.

As gentle waves washed over Amira, she saw Namur cradled in the arms of one mermaid, and Farah in the arms of another, with Layla nuzzling into her sopping hair. She held tight to Semek's bowl.

Leo had done it. He had travelled where no one had been before, trapped the stormbird in eight brass bottles, and stopped it from destroying the Sahar Peninsula.

'We need to go to him!' cried Amira. 'Take us to him!'

The mermaids glanced at one another. And then the the first mermaid spoke.

'He's at the horizon,' she said. 'And how ever will we reach him there?'

Chapter 37

A full day passed before Amira, Farah and the *jinn* saw *Tigerheart* appear at the horizon.

The mermaids had taken them home, as Leo had requested. He had sacrificed himself, just as those on Alhitan had done a thousand years before.

The events that followed Leo's departure were hazy in Amira's memory. That is what grief does to you. It twists your memories, lays a mist over them. So when you march through them again, you lose your way.

Ramady had her kids – two of them. But Amira couldn't understand how life moved on the way it did after you had lost so much.

'Because you have to march on,' Dunya had told her. 'But perhaps not today.'

After Amira had found her mothers safe, and spent an entire evening curled up in their arms, she retreated to her cabin, Namur tucked beside her like always. Except it wasn't like before. Nothing was.

Amira pulled her cards from beneath the pillow. The Lovers, Fool, Death. She thought escaping her fate meant saving Namur, but she had lost Leo in return.

Our lives grow like branches on a tree. They tangle with the lives of others, and stretch far and wide. And we can never guess where they might take us.

Some time later – because Amira had stopped keeping track of the hours, of the rise and fall of the moon – Jamila knocked softly on her door.

'Why does it hurt so much?' asked Amira. It felt as if an egg had hatched in her belly, and a bird was pecking at her insides.

Jamila had been crying too. Amira knew how fond she had become of Leo. She handed Amira a drink.

Amira shook her head. 'I told you I don't want –'

But Jamila pushed the tonic towards her. 'Read the label,' she said.

Amira did. *A tonic to help you understand your feelings.*

After they had returned to the dhow, Farah handed Amira Leo's bag. She had kept it safe, as promised. In the centre of the bag, humming like always, was the sphere ball.

Leo had managed to trap the stormbird's current inside the sphere. And, with it, the remnants of emotions buried for a thousand years. Jamila had used the power of the sphere for good. She had extracted the current, and used it in her mixes, and turned a curse into a cure.

If they were going to stop the stormbird from returning, they needed to make sure people learned how to feel on the outside as well as the inside.

'Sometimes,' said Jamila, after she had explained all of this to Amira, 'we should know when to control our emotions. But most of the time it's better simply to understand them. Right now, it's OK to feel the pain. It's the only way to get through your grief. To remember Leo. And one day,' she added as she left the cabin, 'it won't hurt so much.'

Amira felt as if nothing would ever be right again. But then she looked to Namur, and her mothers, and Farah, and a small part of her knew it might. Semek's bowl sat empty by her window, beside the red radio and Leo's gloves. The fish *jinni* had disappeared the day after they reached *Tigerheart*. Amira chose to believe he had found Leo at the horizon.

Farah knocked on Amira's door.

'Come in,' said Amira. Namur was asleep in her lap. She brushed her hands across his fur for comfort. She felt his warmth and the gentle beating of his heart.

Farah peeked in. Layla peered from beneath her nest of hair too, sticking her forked tongue out.

'It's silly to say,' began Farah, coming in to perch on Amira's bed. 'But I'm sorry.'

Amira's eyes filled with tears again. 'I am too,' she said. And then she surprised herself by saying more; perhaps because Farah had shared so much with her. 'Leo was so brave that day, to just . . .' She couldn't put it into words, not in the way she wanted to.

'I know,' said Farah. From behind her back she pulled out a book. Green cloth, with a golden border. 'That's why we should never forget,' she said. 'To tell our story. Tell *his* story.'

◇✦◇

To the surprise of her mothers Amira entered the main cabin and picked up the bakhoor filled with charcoal. She selected orange-scented wood chips, Leo's smell, and lit them. Then she carried the bakhoor to the table in the middle. Her mothers followed her curiously. So did Ramady and her kids.

Amira danced around the room until smoke from the bakhoor filled the air. Farah, the animals and the *jinn* clustered together as a story formed above them.

Amira picked up her pen. And she wrote on the very first page of the book: *Tales from the Sahar Peninsula*. She turned the page again, and she began to write a story . . .

The Tale of the Boy Who Sang to the Moon

There was once a boy with the voice of a songbird. Despite his gifts, he was rather shy. But when the sky turned dark, and everyone retreated inside their homes, the boy came alive.

Every night he would climb out of his window to the roof of his house, and there he would sing to the moon. Sometimes he would sing songs of love and laughter, joy and fun. Other times he would recite ballads of sadness and woe. But each time he finished his song, the boy would whisper his secrets to the moon and relinquish the worries that weighed on his heart.

And so it happened that he visited the moon every night for four long years.

On the boy's twelfth birthday he didn't climb on to the roof and he didn't serenade the moon. She waited, shining as bright as she could for him. But as the sun began to rise, the moon was forced to turn away, cold and alone.

She returned the next night. But, once again, the boy did not appear.

On the third night the moon mourned. She was sure the boy was gone for good.

She wept bitter tears that spoke of the sadness. And, very slowly, her love turned to rage. She hated the world for snatching the boy away from her, and she vowed to seek revenge.

That night, the tides changed. The sea, full as it was with the moon's tears, rose higher, and higher, and higher still, threatening to flood every village, town and city in the Sahar Peninsular.

The people fled, packed their things and left for the mountains, where they hoped they would be safe. And, in the very corner of one rather big city, the boy felt the moon's rage. He had, just that night, performed his music for adoring crowds that beamed at him as bright as the moon had all those years past.

Realizing the moon was missing him, the boy climbed to the top of the tallest tower and sang her a song of love.

When he was finished, the boy promised he would sing to the moon every fortnight. And so the tides pulled back, and the waves of the sea softened; the people returned to their villages, towns and cities, and the boy returned to his audience.

The moon waited for the boy. But she was as impatient as she was beautiful. On silent nights she cried, the tides slowly rising as she did. But the people weren't afraid any more. Because every twelfth night, the boy would sing once more, and the tides would fall, and they would be safe. All because of a moonchild's voice.

If you ever find the sea as smooth as silk, the waves calm, that's because the boy is there, singing to the moon to grant us all safe passage. Wherever it is we may go.

Chapter 38

Do you know now, who was telling the story? Do you know who spoke of the midnight souk, and Alhitan, of *jinn* and stormbirds? It was me, Amira. I will never stop trying to reach the horizon and Leo.

And while I try, I plan to collect stories and write them down. I plan to find magic and spread it across the world.

And I will always, always keep one eye on the horizon.

THE END

Acknowledgements

Writing this book has been a whirlwind and I'm so thankful for all of the people who came along for the ride. Claire, for your eternal wisdom and guidance; Sarah, for patiently shaping and reshaping this story with me even when we couldn't see the end; and everyone else on the RCW and Egmont teams, especially Miriam, Sam, Liz, Lucy, Laura, Bhavini, Siobhan, Hilary, Jas, Olivia and Jennie R.

Thank you to my friends for letting me panic (over and over again), offering advice, and sharing in my excitement (bonus points to those of you who did all three). I won't name you all because I'll leave someone out and feel bad forever, but you know who you are. A special thanks to my Dana(h)s for sorting out my Arabic, and Soraya for your insight.

To my trio of parents: thank you for your support, past and present.

And always, Alfie, the MVP. Thank you for guiding me every day in every way.

To all of the well-travelled cats I've loved before, from Kuwait to England, for compelling me to write about a child and her cat companion: especially Coco, Kadbury, Koki, BB and Kiki (and Luna for birthing her).

And thank you to the Rentons for bringing Kiki into my life.

A final but very special thank you to Rachael, for bringing this story to life with your stunning, brilliant illustrations. It's as if you saw into my mind but made it better. The children's publishing world is so lucky to have you among their ranks.

The magic continues in the next

MOONCHILD

book, coming soon!

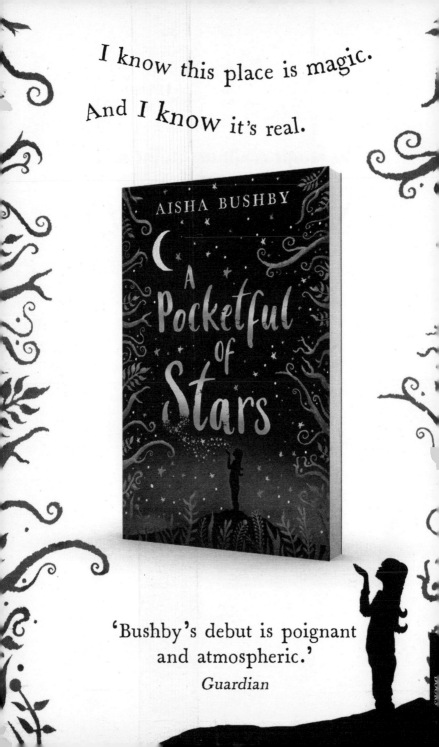